THEY STOLE FROM ME

THE CULPRITS

Julian Hajar. Commercial director.

Julian was in his early fifties, with a good head of white hair, Around six feet tall and quite a bit overweight. It seemed he was fond of the good life. He always managed to look scruffy, wearing trousers that could have done with being an inch longer and badly ironed shirts. Julian didn't lack confidence and had a big ego. Whatever anyone talked about, he had a bigger and better story. If someone had seen the pope, Julian would have had an audience with the pope. Another issue was that he would only half listen to other people's views, always itching to get his own opinion across. He liked the sound of his own voice and was guilty of repeating anecdotes. Julian considered himself to be quite the entertainer, often attempting to impersonate the comedian Michael McIntyre in his attempts to tell funny stories. Julien wasn't a board director. He managed to convince the company, that having the word director on his business cards, would somehow have a bigger impact on potential clients. His role was to secure new projects and develop the business.

Steve Ginn. Surveying director.

Steve was closing in on retirement, having worked with the same company for over forty years. He was part of the furniture and in a very comfortable position. Quite a comical little fellow with thinning grey hair and a big red nose. Steve dressed a bit casually for a director but none of the board seemed to mind. He was a bit of a sit on the fence type of character, trying to keep everyone happy. When under pressure he tended to mumble and stutter. Like a politician, not answering a question. Many of his stories revolved around holidays with his wife and always including Steve ending up so drunk that he couldn't remember too much about any of the locations he had visited. This went a long way to explain his red nose. Steve's role was to control the purse strings of all the quantity surveyors in the company.

Brian Rice. Construction director.

Brian was an ex-fire fighter who joined the company as a site manager. Within three years he had been promoted to the level of construction director. This rapid rise can be attributed to the fact Brian's father was best pals with the company owner and managing director. He was in his early forties, well-built and always very smartly dressed. Brian walked about the office as if he owned the place and was unpopular with much of the workforce. He was balding, so kept his hair shaved close to his head, giving him a menacing look. All in all, Brian was a bully, who used his position to get rid of anyone that went against him. His role was to ensure all sites adhered meticulously to health and safety regulations.

THE VICTIM

Jack Watson. Contracts manager.

Jack was physically abused by his father and ignored by his alcoholic mother. He spent his early teens in and out of care homes. Then he ended up with the wrong crowd. Jack spent years in borstal and mainstream prisons for a range of crimes.

At twenty-two he met the woman of his dreams and this transformed his life. Jack studied hard and became a construction site manager and spent many successful years progressing well and earning decent money.

CHAPTER 1

Jack is thirty-three and is the happiest he has ever been. For years he had fought the demons from his childhood. Now he believes the past is locked in the past, where he hoped it would remain.

At the age of twenty-six Jack married Laura. He absolutely cherished the ground she walked on. Her beauty took his breath away every day. Laura is petite and weighs around fifty-five kilos. Her hair is flaming red but Jack is most besotted by her piercing green eyes and perfect smile. They are lovers and best friends.

They have a son, Robbie (named after Laura's grandfather) who is three and quite a handful. The one thing Jack would insure was, his son would not endure the pain he had suffered at the hands of his own parents.

Laura worshipped Jack. His curly blonde hair which always looked a bit unkempt. His broad muscular shoulders and the way he stood tall and proud. She referred to him as "my handsome man." One of her favourite things was the way he walked, very confidently, almost cocky. For the most part though she was lost in his big blue eyes.

Life was good for the Watson family. They had bought a spacious two-bedroom house in Hertfordshire, not too far from London and ideal for bringing up a child. The river Lea was on their doorstep. The happy couple spent two years decorating and furnishing it to their taste. They were truly content and the envy of many of their friends.

What made them so happy was that they always discussed things before making any decisions. The plan was to buy a bigger house and extend the family. Laura had returned to work as a credit control manager. All of her income was added to their savings each month.

Jack had been with the same construction company for five years and he was doing very well. A valuable member of the team, or so one of the directors had said. Both Jack and Laura thought it was high time he was promoted to contracts manager, a natural progression on his career path. An appraisal meeting was due and that would be the perfect opportunity for Jack to broach this subject.

Unfortunately, the appraisal didn't pan out as Jack had hoped. The company were delighted with his performance but considered it a little early for him to make the leap into contracts management. They promised to review this in a years' time.

Jack was a little bit down when he broke the news to Laura, however she was as supportive as ever and told him "The company had made a big error. Look for a new company Jack, one that will appreciate you, and see your potential." The search began, Jack signed up with a few recruitment agencies and updated his CV. He didn't hand in his notice at work. They considered it best to wait until he had a concrete job offer first.

Jack was very excited about taking on a new challenge. He was very confident in his own ability and felt he had been doing the role of a contracts manager for the past year.

CHAPTER 2

It only took a month and three applications, for Jack to be invited to attend an interview for the role of contracts manager. The company was based in Hertfordshire, about a thirty-minute drive from where he lived. STG services. They were predominantly a plumbing and heating contractor but had moved into construction in the past five years. The salary on offer was more than Jack's current income, but a little on the low side for a contracts manager. Both Laura and Jack thought there was nothing to lose by attending the interview.

Jack was calm as he pulled into the car park at STG offices. He hadn't been for an interview in six years, in his mind he was a shoe in to get the job.

Jack was interviewed by Julian Hajar and Richard Black. The first thing that struck him was the big mop of white hair that Julian wore in a centre parting. Richard was the current contracts manager who was leaving the company. He had bought a bed and breakfast in Torquay and was setting up in business with his wife. The interview went very well, Jack thought he had made a good impression as he answered all their questions without hesitation.

A week later, STG invited Jack for a second interview. This time with the company owner Adam Truss, and a senior director, Steve Ginn.
Laura was so proud of her handsome man; they shared a couple of glasses of wine to celebrate what they considered

to be a formality. Jack said, "I will walk in holding a pen, and ask where I sign". "Don't you dare you cocky bugger," laughed Laura.

Jack was greeted by Steve Ginn for his second interview. Basically, for twenty minutes he talked about the company's history, and goals. Then a youngish man in a very smart suit came in and introduced himself as Adam, the M.D. Jack was surprised as Adam appeared to be younger than him. After a brief chat Jack was offered the position with STG and accepted on the spot, explaining he would need to work his one month's notice with his currant employers.

Jack phoned Laura with the news she fully expected to hear, and a celebration was planned for that evening.

His boss was shocked and visibly annoyed when Jack handed in his notice.

On his way home he stopped off to buy a bottle of Moet, although he didn't really care much for the stuff, Laura would love it. When Jack walked in, little Robbie was at the table in his highchair, munching on something that looked gross. Laura came in from the kitchen carrying two steak dinners. She was wearing Jacks favourite dress. Both had tears of happiness as they embraced. Jack popped the champagne, causing Robbie to jump. They raised their glasses and Laura said, "Here's to the beginning of a new chapter. Congratulations my handsome man."

CHAPTER 3

Jack aged nine.

As jack approached his home, a two-bedroom ground floor flat on a council estate in Hackney, He was filled with trepidation. Will his mum be sober? Will his dad be in a bad mood? Both of his parents were claiming benefits, Jack never knew them to have jobs. Dad was a gambler; the results of the day determined his mood. He was in poor health for a man of forty-five, clearly overweight and smoked like a chimney. He was always dreaming of that one big win that would change their lives. Jack doubted that anything would ever change. His mum was two years older and had been an alcoholic for years, Jack had no memory of her being sober. Vodka was her favourite, but anything would do in a crisis. Jack wished he had a sibling, but no, he was alone in his anguish. He never brought friends back to the flat, not that he would have been allowed even if he wanted to. He lied to his school friends that his dad was a businessman and his mum a chemist, they didn't believe him.

As he opened the door, he could hear the telly blaring, and muffled laughter coming from the front room. At least they seem to be in a good mood, he thought to himself.
"Hi mum, hi dad." Jack tried to sound cheerful as he entered the room. Both parents barely acknowledged him, just a couple of grunts.

There was never any dinner prepared and hardly any food in the flat. Jack had some cornflakes for his dinner, the same as for breakfast. Once he finished, jack washed his bowl, as he was drying it the bowl slipped from his hands and smashed on the floor. Jack stood there frozen in shear panic. The door to the kitchen flew open, His red-faced dad came charging in, calling him all the names under the sun. "Clean it up you little shit, do you think we are made of money." As he swept up the mess his dad hit him with a belt twice across his back, another beating he thought. As he looked up, he saw his mum at the kitchen door, laughing.

"Go to your room and don't come down until morning. I'm sick of looking at your pathetic face." His dad roared. His mum laughed louder. Another night alone for Jack, scared and hungry.

The next day at school, during sports, a teacher noticed bruises on Jacks arm. She took him to one side and asked. "What happened to your arm Jack."

"Oh, it's nothing miss, I'm a bit clumsy, always bumping into things."

She wasn't convinced but advised Jack to be more careful. The incident played on her mind so much that Ms Walsh reported it to the headmaster Mr Young, who suggested she kept a close eye on Master Watson. If there were any more bruises, social services would have to be alerted.

CHAPTER 4

Now.

Jack opted for a company car as part of his package, so on his first day at his new place of work he needed a lift. Laura was extremely happy to oblige. Jack started at eight o' clock. Laura Parked outside STG offices at seven thirty, Robbie, sitting in the back was enjoying the music from the car radio, happily tapping his little feet. Jack gave Laura a big kiss on the lips and got out of the car. She watched him as he walked towards the glass fronted entrance. She thought how smart he looked. He was wearing dark blue Polo trousers and black loafers, a blue gingham checked shirt, set off by a pink tie. In his previous job, Jack wore cargo pants and work boots along with sweatshirts bearing the company logo. This was a different world. She was close to tears as she watched her handsome man. Laura couldn't have been prouder.

"Knock them bandy darling." She shouted.

Jack gave a big smile and saluted his wife and child before disappearing into the building.

There was nobody at the reception desk so Jack sat down in the waiting area. A few minutes later a young girl came rushing in obviously a bit late, she looked flustered as she asked, "How can I help?"

Jack explained this was his first day and he was here to meet Steve Ginn. "I'll tell him you're here," she said cheerfully. "And welcome to our company." Jack thanked her.

Steve greeted him with a warm handshake and a big smile, then led him upstairs to the office he shared with Julian, who was already at his desk. Another warm handshake and welcoming smile. This was followed by an offer of tea or coffee and small talk about the weekend. Julian had been fishing, and Steve had guests over on Saturday night. He joked that he couldn't remember too much about It, so it must have been good. As he told his story he raised both hands and did the inverted commas sign with his fingers, at that point Julian raised an imaginary gun and shot him. They both laughed loudly. Steve explained that every time he made that gesture, again demonstrating the motion. Julian thought he looked like a squirrel so shot him; more laughter followed from the chuckle brothers. Jack laughed along even though he thought it was pathetic.

Julian then laid out the agenda for Jacks first day. At nine o'clock HR would run him through all the company policies and protocols and give him an induction. Richard, the outgoing contracts manager would then take him to the office where he would be based, in Waltham Abby. Great thought Jack, even closer to home. Richard was due at around ten o' clock.

It took nearly an hour to finish with HR, Jack thought it was all a bit much to take in but smiled and nodded anyway. He was told he had a half day holiday which would have to be used at some point during the week or be lost. The carrying over of holidays was not permitted. This completely baffled Jack.

Richard was waiting when Jack got back to Steve's office. After the formalities they set off to Waltham Abby.
It was only a twenty-minute drive between the two offices. The time was filled with Richard waxing lyrical about

his new life which was about to start in Torquay. Apparently, he had dreamt of owning a bed and breakfast for many years but just never had the balls to go for it. He had remarried five years previously and he said it was his new wife's encouragement and financial involvement that was the final push he needed.

The office in Waltham Abbey was in a modern building housing a multitude of companies. STG had rented two units on the second floor; one was reserved purely for meetings. The main area had four desks, each had a large flat screen monitor and keyboard along with a telephone, only one was occupied. Jack was introduced to Trish, the company's buyer. She looked to be in her Early thirties and seemed friendly enough. Jack thought she looked a little stressed. Although the office felt warm to Jack, He was in his shirt sleeves, Trish was wearing a baggy sweater with a matching woolly hat and fingerless gloves. Jack asked.

"Are you not feeling well?" Trish mumbled something about the air conditioning being crap, without averting her eyes from her screen. Richard raised his eyebrows and mouthed "Women's trouble." Using his fingers to make the inverted comma sign. Jack thought this was a bit sexist. Richard explained the empty desks, one was his, the second, opposite from Trish belonged to John France, The mechanical and electrical manager. He had booked the day off to play golf. The other was where the Quantity surveyor Barry Shanklin sat, he too had booked a day off.

Richard said that he had some calls to catch up on and handed Jack a batch of four lever-arch files which contained all the information on the sites Jack was responsible for.

"Have a flick through those and make a few notes, I will take you to all the sites after lunch." Jack sat at Johns desk, knowing he would inherit Richards seat once he had packed his bags and set off into the Torquay sunset.

This was a completely new situation for Jack as he was used to being on sites, not in an office environment, he felt a little awkward. Trish stood up and said, "Come on Jack, I will show you around." She took him to a fully stocked kitchen/dining area with plenty of seating. Jack was used to having his food sat in metal containers, this is great he thought. She then gave him his entry fob and showed him the toilet area which had showers. Jack was amazed and couldn't wait to tell Laura. Back at his desk, time dragged as he looked at drawings and specifications for the various sites. At one thirty Richard said "Come on Jack look lively, we are off. We need to be back at Potters Bar to pick up your car at five o' clock." Jack didn't know what make of company car he was getting but was very excited none the less.

CHAPTER 5

There first stop was a block of four houses in Epping, Richard stated that these were nearing completion and should be handed over in six weeks. Jack was introduced to the on-site manager; Andrew, who was a few years younger than Jack. Richard had some more calls to make so he left it to Andrew to show Jack around. One of the houses was complete and that's where the tour started. Jack wasn't too impressed with the quality of the product but was informed that the client had accepted this as a benchmark. Andrew also relayed that there were several issues and constraints slowing up the finishing of the project. The procurement of materials was the most frustrating, closely followed by sub-contractors not showing up when booked, because of overdue payments for valuations. Great thought Jack. There was a further concern, which was Epping council, the client had a zero-tolerance policy when it came to asbestos in the soil around the properties. An asbestos survey had been carried out and hotspots identified and removed. A further test was required on completion. The site had a water course to the rear of the gardens, Jack noticed old garage roofing sheets dumped in the area. Alarm bells started to ring and it wasn't even two o' clock on his first day.

The next site was in Hemel Hempstead, about a forty-five-minute drive. Richard was more interested in talking about Torquay, rather than asbestos, so Jack just listened and nodded at the right times. The site manager in Hemel was George. Who is in his fifties, but he came across as being very enthusiastic, a bit like Jack was when he started. The project consisted of four three-bedroom houses for social housing. The foundations were done but there was no labour on site. George explained the bricks were not ordered in time and were not due for another six weeks. George shook his head, clearly despondent. He asked Richard was there any other part of the contract that could be started while waiting for the bricks. He just shook his head and walked outside to answer his phone. Jack told George he would review the program and come to site later in the week with a plan of attack. This seemed to placate George somewhat. The final site was in Luton, a short distance away. A smaller site with only three houses. This was in the same situation as Hemel, foundations were done but the bricks and blocks hadn't been ordered. Richard opened the site and showed Jack around, this took all of five minutes. On the drive back to Potters bar to collect Jacks new car, he asked Richard what the clients reaction was to the six-week delays. Richard laughed "We told them there was a country wide shortage for that particular brick and planning wouldn't accept any alternative." They had approved an extension of time to the contract program.

Jack's company car was waiting in the car park. It was a Ford Mondeo, which would do nicely thought Jack.

Laura met Jack at the front door, with a big smile and open arms. She said,
"How was your first day my handsome man?"
Jack nestled into her arms and replied,
"Not quite what I expected."

CHAPTER 6

Jack aged 12.

Jack was now at secondary school and had made some new friends, but generally he preferred to keep himself to himself. He always refused invitations to fellow pupils homes so he could avoid inviting anyone to the flat he still lived in with his parents.

The beatings had continued but Jack managed to hide the bruises from his teachers. His previous school had notified social services and Jack was on the at-risk register.

On his journey home, Jack was as usual feeling increasingly anxious the closer he got to the flat. The abuse wasn't daily but at least once a week, when his old man had lost at the bookies. As he opened the door the smell of smoke was strong, he could see it was coming from the kitchen. Jack covered his mouth with his sleeve and rushed in and using a tea towel he removed the burning pot from the stove. There were no flames, just smoke. In the pot were two eggs, both had exploded. He opened the window and ran into the front room, as usual the TV was blaring. His mum was sprawled out on the settee holding a bottle of vodka which was three quarters empty. She was dribbling and groaning. "God mum." Jack yelled. "You could have killed yourself." No response. Jack took the bottle of vodka and the tears were streaming down his face as he poured the remaining contents down the kitchen sink.

"What the fuck are you doing Jack?" His mother screamed as she raced into the kitchen.

"Give me that bottle." Jack managed to hold her off until the last drop was gone. He then handed it to his mother. Jack was now sobbing.

"I love you mum." She was furious and lashed out at Jack, forgetting she had the bottle in her hand. She struck him across the side of the head, Jack screamed as the bottle shattered sending glass all over the kitchen. Blood poured from the gash by Jacks temple. His mum snapped out of her rage and the realisation of what she had done hit home. She grabbed her son and cried "I'm sorry darling. I didn't mean it." She held Jack close; both were crying now.

The shock had sobered her up and she knew she had to think quickly.

"Listen Jack, I need to call an ambulance for you, that cut is pretty deep and might need a few stitches." Jack just nodded. "You need to tell them you slipped and hit your head on the corner of the table." Jack looked confused.

"If you don't, they will take mummy away and you will be put in a home, do you want that, Jack?"

"No mum."

"Then do as I say, hold this towel on your head tightly while I clean up this mess."

When the paramedics arrived, the kitchen was clean, apart from some areas of blood splatters and a convenient smear on the corner of the table. Jacks mother had dressed and put on some make up. The first thing they noticed was the smell of smoke.

"Who's been burning the toast?" One of the paramedics joked, trying to lighten the mood.

"He's in the kitchen." said Jacks mother.

Jack was sitting at the table holding the towel as instructed.

"What happened to you then soldier?"

"I forgot about the pot on the hob, when I saw the smoke, I rushed in to turn off the gas and tripped and hit my head on the table." Jack blurted, almost too scripted.

"Ok let's take a look."

The gash was about five centimetres long. The paramedic saw something sparkle in the cut; he knew the lad was lying. He also noticed some shards of glass under the table.

"You need to get him a fresh shirt for after they treat him at the hospital." He told Jacks mother. She did as he said. Before the paramedics arrived, she had phoned her husband and told him the story. Jack and his mother got into the back of the ambulance and were taken the short journey to the local hospital.

At the hospital, Jack was taken into a treatment room on arrival. One of the paramedics had rang ahead and informed the doctor of his suspicions. Both social services and the police had been called and would be at the hospital imminently. Jacks mother was told to sit in the relatives waiting room.

"But I want to be with my son." She protested. The nurse tried to calm her down and explained that this was normal procedure. She shook her head and sat down in a huff.

Jack's father came into the waiting room some twenty minutes later.

"That little shit had better stick to the story or your fucked my dear." He blurted.

"We will both be fucked you idiot, you're the one that keeps beating him, if they see the bruises, there are bound to be questions." They sat waiting in silence.

The police cautioned and arrested both parents.

Jack had broken down and told the truth about what had happened. He admitted that he was regularly beaten by his father which explained the bruises to his chest and arms.

Jack was taken into care. Both parents ended up with jail sentences and were given restraining orders, preventing them from seeing or even contacting Jack.

CHAPTER 7

Now.

Jack got to his office at seven thirty. John and Barry were already there, drinking tea and merrily chatting away. After the introductions and some small talk, Jack told them he wanted a meeting with his team at two o' clock that afternoon. Mainly to discuss programs, Procurements and sub-contract orders. John and Barry agreed it was a good idea. The boys carried on chatting, it seemed they were good mates. John was talking about his new hobby golf, and Barry about stock car racing.

At eight o'clock, Jack took himself off to the meeting room, which housed a printer. He explained he had several drawings and programs to print out.

Trish, it appeared didn't start until nine o'clock.

Jack spent all morning going through the programs for the various sites, he immediately saw opportunities to shorten the durations, when he did his own construction programs. There wasn't much in the way of sub-contract orders, only the ones for bricklaying and scaffolding had been placed. This seemed odd to Jack, He would address this at the meeting later.

At one o' clock, Jack went to the dining area to heat up the lunch that Laura had prepared the night before. Chili Con Carne, one of Jacks favourites. Bless her, she had packed it in a heart shaped box. The area was busy, with mostly young girls gossiping away. Jack always had an eye for a pretty girl but his head was not for turning, not now he had found the love of his life.

When Jack walked into the meeting room, Trish, John and Barry were already sitting with note pads opened. Starting with Trish, each laid out their roles within the company, it seems there was very little definition to Trish and Barry's remits, their roles overlapped. John oversaw all the heating and plumbing elements. He told Jack that STG had used in-house plumbers for the three new build projects that had been completed. This caused problems with programming because planned maintenance work, which was the companies bread and butter, took priority. They were planning to move over to using sub-contractors for future new build projects.

To Jacks mind, this was the only way forward.

The meeting went on for over two hours and Jack was getting increasingly agitated by the lack of energy in the team. No materials had been procured and most of the sub-contract packages hadn't even been sent out for pricing.

Jack told them this was unacceptable and things would have to change. Trish mentioned that she was the only buyer and although Barry helped, she was struggling. Jack told her he would set up a procurement schedule giving precise dates when materials would be needed on all sites. She acknowledged that this would be a huge help. He told Barry that he would do the same for when the sub-contract packages needed to be placed. Jack couldn't believe that there had been no pre-start meetings for the two packages already in the file. He again highlighted that this was unacceptable and would have to change. The mood in the room was a bit frosty, so Jack wrapped it up and thanked the three of them.

When they got back to their desks, John said.

"Who does he think he is? He has only been here a couple of days and he thinks he is running the bloody company." The other two laughed.

"He won't last long. We have seen his type before. They never do." Added Barry Again, all three laughed.

"I think he has some good ideas. He could be the breath of fresh air this company needs." Trish said.

On the short drive home, Jack wondered if he had made a mistake by joining STG. He decided to keep this from Laura as he didn't want her to worry. This wasn't like Jack; in recent years he had learnt not to bottle things up.

CHAPTER 8

Jack spent the next two days on site with the managers. Talking through their concerns and what he could do to make their jobs easier. He got input from them for the new construction programs. But it was Jack who was calling the shots. On the two projects that were waiting for bricks, Jack decided he could bring forward the fencing and land scaping to the rear of the properties, which was shown at the end of the programs. He arranged a meeting with the team for Friday morning. Julian and Steve accepted their invitations.

They met in the meeting room at Potters Bar. Jack was there early and had laid out an agenda, procurement schedules and programs for all his projects. John was the first to arrive, closely followed by the chuckle brothers Julian and Steve.

"Where is Barry?" Asked Jack.

"He had to go to Epping to check on the clients snagging list." Said Steve.

Jack was baffled by this.

"Why is the quantity surveyor doing snagging? That's what we have site managers for."

"Oh, it's just something he has always done." Added Steve.

"Well perhaps he should be focussing on the job he is paid to do and we wouldn't be in this mess." Jack said shaking his head. The room went quiet. Jack went through his plans to finish the projects earlier than programmed and insisted that the only way it work was if the whole team bought into it. Julian was extremely impressed and Steve thought his procurement schedule was brilliant. Jack emphasised the importance of getting the sub-contract orders out early and detailed the value in having pre-start meetings. These made life easier for the surveyors. Steve admitted it was something that STG hadn't done in the past but he could see the benefits. John didn't have input, Jack wondered why he was even there.

They also thought doing the fencing was a clever idea as the sites were idle. Finally, Jack mentioned that the completed show house in Epping was different to the CGI (computer generated image)

"What do you mean different Jack?"

He told them the CGI showed a hard wood handrail and Mahogany was clearly stated in the specification.

"What have we got?" asked Julian.

Jack told them that the handrail was soft wood and had been painted white. All three shook their heads in disbelief.

"So much for Barry the snagger" Jack laughed.

The two directors decided it was best not to mention this to the client and hope for the best. Very professional thought Jack.

After the meeting Jack rang Barry and arranged to meet him at two-thirty in the office at Waltham Abby. He also told Trish to be available. Trish thought the list of dates jack had drawn up was fantastic, now she could place orders well in advance and tick them off on a tracker. Jack told her that if she had any queries with quantities, he would be happy to help. She looked a very happy girl.

"Right, we have a date for the brick deliveries, when are the blocks due?"

"Nobody asked me to order the blocks yet."

"You're kidding me." Jack said alarmed by this.

She went on to say that her background was not in construction, which is why the schedule would be such a great help. Jack thanked Trish and said she could return to her work.

"OK Barry, what do you make of your list?"

"Yeah, it's great, I might struggle to meet some of the early dates. I have a lot on."

"As I explained to Julian and Steve, we all have to buy into this for it to be a success."

Jack asked Barry what the scaffolder had included for in his quote.

"Four lifts to the perimeter of the building"

"What, no loading bay?"

"No."

"And no internal scaffold?"

"No, we always use Band stands and hop ups."

"Not anymore, arrange a meeting with the scaffolder to re-quote." It was clear Barry wasn't happy with this but agreed to set it up for early next week.

"Question for you." Barry said.

"What are window formers?"

"You're shitting me."

"No, I have never heard of them."

Jack explained what they were and the importance installing them as the brickwork goes up to ensure that the windows will fit.

"Well, we have never used them before," Barry grumbled. Jack was getting tired of hearing this excuse. He walked over to the window and called Barry over.

"There is a reason I drive that car." Jack said pointing to the car park.

"And not a horse and cart, it's called progress Barry. This company needs to drag its arse out of the eighties and catch up with the rest of the world." Trish burst out laughing and said,

"He has a point." Barry was red faced when he walked out of the office.

Jack decided to get a quote for the window formers for the project in Hemel which consisted of forty windows. To his surprise the windows had been ordered, so he contacted that company and they sent there quote back in a couple of hours.

Jack gave Barry the quote, before the site meeting with the scaffolder. He couldn't believe the amount and said he would place the order. Jack told him to order the formers for the Luton project.
"Don't you worry Jack; I will be ordering them for all jobs in the future. Progress, right?"
Jack smiled at this minor victory, but felt an uphill journey lay ahead.

Jack had discussed the scaffold requirements with the bricklayer and he was told that there was no need for loading bays.

The scaffold contractor wanted an extra eight hundred pound to instal an internal platform. By the look on His face, you would think he had asked Barry to shoot his grandmother.

"I'll have to run it by Steve and let you know later." This annoyed Jack, he couldn't believe how a surveyor didn't have the balls to accept the new price. Barry could see that Jack was not impressed. Jack left without saying anything and headed to Hemel.

On The drive Jacks phone rang, Steve. Well, I wonder what he wants Jack thought. With a wry smile he pressed the hands-free button.

"Hi Steve, how's it going?"

"All good, Barry says you want to spend an extra eight hundred quid on scaffold?"

"Yes, Steve it' a no brainer,"

"Can you explain please, this is something we don't usually do?"

"Just trust me on this one Steve. I will get a discount from the bricklayer and knock two weeks off the program."

"Really? That's great, go for it mate."

CHAPTER 9

Jack aged fourteen.

Over the past two years, Jack had lived with four different foster parents, and changed schools three times. He felt he didn't fit in anywhere. Each of the families he stayed with were caring enough. The first two were similar, both in their thirties and unable to have children of their own. They molly coddled Jack, wrapped him up in cotton wool, called the doctor at the first sign of a sniffle. Jack felt as though he was six years old, he couldn't bear all the pampering. The third family, Jack felt only did it for the money.

They let him go and do whatever he wanted, Jack was hardly in school, so social services took him back into care. The fourth family had two children both teenage boys. They resented the fact that Jack was given preferential treatment and bullied him constantly. It got too much for Jack, one day he snapped and punched both, causing blood and tears.

Back in care, Jack was getting more and more withdrawn, never joining in with any of the activities which were on offer daily. Counselling was considered but it was decided Jack was a little too young and this could confuse him even more.

Jack was taken to his next foster home, in Tottenham, North London. A couple in their fifties whose own children had flown the nest.
He was welcomed by a very cheery Peter and Joanne, who preferred to be called Jo.

"Come in son, welcome to our little palace." Peter said in a cockney accent. The word son made Jack feel warm inside. This was something his own father never called him.

"Take a pew son, no need to stand on ceremony in my gaff."

Jack sat down smiling. He liked Peter already.

"Don't get your hopes up yet." He told himself.

After Jo had shown Jack his bedroom, the social worker left them to it.

"Right son, I want you to take us as you find us, this is your home now and we hope you will be happy here. There are no rules as such. We eat together every evening and chat about the day.

If you're hungry or thirsty just help yourself, there is no need to wait to be asked. All we ask is that you wash up after yourself, keep your room tidy and put your dirty clothes in the bathroom laundry basket." Jack sat there nodding, inside he felt like never before. He really liked these people.

Jack preyed that nothing would go wrong.

Jo smiled at Jack.

"We are going to get on like a house on fire."

The change in Jack over the next three months was amazing. Peter had his own bespoke carpentry company. Designing and making furniture to order from the massive shed he had built in the garden. Jack couldn't wait to get home from school to help Peter. The deal was Jack had to do his homework first, no problem he did it with a smile. His grades had been gradually going up, which made Jo very proud. On weekends Peter took Jack to the jobs so he could help and see the installed product. For his efforts of a couple of hours a night and most Saturdays Peter gave Jack a hundred pounds per week in his own pay packet. He had never seen, let alone held that much money. He opened a junior savings account at the local building society. Jo just loved the bond between them, it was like Peter had a third child.

Jack got the best Christmas present he ever had. A carpenters tool belt along with tools to put in it. He was so proud, walking into the shed with his hammer, cordless drill and tape measure in his brown leather tool belt. Jo had put a carpenters pencil behind Jacks ear.

"Now you look like a mini-Peter."

Peter noticed a little swagger as Jack walked in.

"Look at you my little apprentice. Come on son let's make a joiner out of you."

Jack could not have been any happier, his cheeks hurt from smiling so much. For the first time in his life, he felt loved and welcomed.

CHAPTER 10

Now.

Jack had been with STG for over two months and he felt he was slowly winning the battle. His line managers, Steve and Julian were certainly impressed and buying into the changes Jack had implemented. Trish was a different buyer now, organised and confident. She was prone to bouts of illness and took a lot of time off, this didn't bode well with senior management. Jack had heard whispers that she would be gone in a month.

A chain is only as strong as its weakest link. Jack's chain had two weak links. John was still trying to use in house plumbers. He thought he could save the company money this way. No matter how hard Jack tried to convince him that delays to programs would cost a lot more in the long term, John was too short sighted. He would just stroll around the office swinging an imaginary golf club and looking into the distance as it he had hit one straight down the middle. Another of Johns traits was to hum and sing Christmas carols even though it was June. It made Jacks blood boil every time he heard.

"And a partridge in a pear tree."

The other weak link was Barry. He had missed all but one of the dates on the list Jack drew up in his first week. That was for the timber floors and roof trusses. The only reason this was in place was because Jack got a carpentry company, he had used many times in the past to quote for the work. Barry still maintained he was too busy. He was only too busy because he was still doing jobs outside of his remit. He was interfering with the buying, when there was no need, as Trish was on top of everything. It was clear that Barry wanted to be the golden boy. Always the first one in the office and last to leave. Busy being busy.

Jack saw how he wasted time. Trish was off sick and Jack needed to order four timber garden fence posts for the Epping contract, which was nearing completion. All the houses were finished and handed over to a delighted client. Only the externals remained. Barry said he would resource the fence posts. Jack was working at his computer and could hear Barry talking to several different builders merchants, trying to get the best deal. It took him three hours to place the order and he only managed to save twenty pounds. There was an atmosphere developing between Jack and Barry.

Jack was interrupted by John, alias Tiger Woods.

"We are doing a competition for the football world cup. Five pounds to enter. Do you fancy having a go?"

"Sure, put my name down." John explained that all he needed to do was predict the scores to all the matches throughout the tournament. Three points for a correct score and one point for a correct result. Prizes for first, second and third.

Jack raised his concerns about Barry to Julian. He knew this may be risky but was worried about hitting targets he had assured clients he would meet. Julian said that because Barry had been with the company for over ten years, he had become set in his ways and was finding it difficult to adapt to my fast pace. Jack suggested that maybe STG needed to employ another Surveyor. Or at least an assistant to help Barry. Julian just waffled on.

"It will be better on future projects; we can have all the schedules in place before they start." Jack felt he was being fobbed off.

"When we are late with the present contracts and hit with penalties, where will the finger of blame be directed? Yes me, The team leader."

Jack's tone was very serious.

"No, we don't have a blame culture here, we are a team. If we sink or swim, we, do it together."

Jack shook his head and left Julian's office thinking what a crock of shit that was.

CHAPTER 11

Jack had got the results of the asbestos tests back, and the news was not good. He arranged an emergency meeting with the team. Not surprisingly Barry and John failed to attend, still too busy being busy.

Jack emphasised the seriousness of the situation. The results showed 0.1.F/M3. Point one asbestos fibres per cubic centimetre of air. This was an acceptable level in every borough in London, except Epping. Jack had spoken to several departments at Epping council but they would not budge from their zero-tolerance rule, pointing out it was in the contract. Both Julian and Steve looked alarmed.

"What are our options Jack?" asked Julian. Jack told them there were two ways to try to resolve the issue, neither would be cheap.

One was to remove the hotspots recorded on drawings, by the company that carried out the tests. Once the new topsoil had be transported, another test would have to be carried out. Because of the proximity of asbestos around the water tracks, Jack said there were no guarantees of a successful test. The second option, which would be far more expensive, was to remove all the soil from the four gardens and pay extra to have certified topsoil imported by a licenced contractor. A representative from Epping council would have to witness this procedure.

"What do you think Jack?" asked a concerned looking Steve.

"Option two is the only way we can put this to bed timorously."

"I will have to put a cost to this and get a decision from the board." Steve added.

"I'll hold fire from giving the results to the client. He phones me every day on this."

Barry and John did bother to turn up for the afternoons projects review meeting.
"Hello strangers." Jack welcomed them, sarcastically. Neither smiled.

Jack chaired the meeting. Both the Hemel and Luton projects were ahead of the revised programs. He couldn't help but gloat as he mentioned that this was mainly due to using internal scaffolding and window formers. Barry reluctantly agreed this to be the case. Jack again expressed his concerns about the delays in placing the sub-contract orders. Barry claimed to be doing his best. It was agreed that Steve would assist with this in the coming weeks. The decision on the Epping asbestos issue was to remove all the contaminated topsoil and replace it with certified topsoil. This was a considerable cost to the company but Barry announced that the project would still make a twelve percent profit.

Jack stated that he wanted another project review in two weeks, not the usual four.
"I need to keep an eye on sub-contract packages." Jack said looking directly at Barry.
Meeting over.

CHAPTER 12

Jack aged sixteen.

Jack had done well in his GCSE exams. Achieving B's in maths, English and history, along with C's in science and economics. Both Peter and Jo were thrilled and encouraged Jack to stay on at school to do his A levels, and maybe go on to university. Jack had other ideas. He enjoyed carpentry so much that he wanted to follow Peter into the business. In the past two years he had gained many skills and a vast amount of knowledge. After a family discussion it was agreed that Jack would join the business as an apprentice and sign up for an NVQ course in carpentry and joinery. One of the many good things about Peter and Jo was that they listened to what Jack had to say.

"I'm not getting any younger, so I'll need someone to take over the company one day." Peter laughed.

"Rubbish your as fit as a fiddle." Replied Jack.

"We will be partners for years."

Jack got an unexpected email from social services, notifying him that his uncle George (His mother's brother) wanted to get in touch with him. The email contained contact details for George. He told Peter and Jo about the email and as always, they asked Jack what he wanted to do, without trying to influence his decision.

Jack said he had always got on well with George and decided to reply to the email.

Jack met George, as arranged in a café on Seven sisters road. Peter had offered to come along, Jack thanked him and said he would rather go alone. When Jack walked in, he spotted his uncle straight away, the likeness to his mother was striking. They shared a pot of tea and chatted about this and that, how much Jack had grown, blah blah.

"What is the real reason for wanting to see me uncle?"

"There are no flies on you young man." George said with a smile.

"I'm afraid it's bad news. I'm sorry Jack your dad is dead. He lost his two-year battle with lung cancer." Jack sat expressionless as he listened.

"Well, he can't hurt anyone else now, can he? Good riddance to bad rubbish I say."

George was a little taken aback by Jacks coldness but understood.

"What about her?"

"You mean your mum?"

"Your sister, she is not my mum anymore."

"She is in a care home Jack; she has early Alzheimer's brought on by years of excessive alcohol abuse. She doesn't know who I am."

"Good enough for her as well, she did it to herself. They are both dead to me anyway." Again, Jack was emotionless. He thanked his uncle for going through the effort to contact him but asked George not to get in touch again. George nodded in agreement, shook Jacks hand and left.

Jack didn't have many mates; he saw a few school friends now and then. He much preferred to work alongside Peter, they made a great team. They did many things as a family. Jack's favourite was going to watch Tottenham Hotspur play at White Hart Lane. All three had a season ticket. Jack was a West Ham fan as a kid. He found it easy to change allegiance. His life in Hackney was fast becoming a diminishing memory. Jack asked Peter and Jo if he could call them mum and dad. Both cried tears of happiness and held Jack close.

"Of course you can son."

CHAPTER 13

Now.

Jack was on site to oversee the contaminated topsoil being removed, along with the client. This took four hours. Luckly the new asbestos free soil was waiting and was laid in an hour.

Jack immediately produced the handover documents which were signed off by the client.

About time. Thought Jack, at last, I can forget about this project.

"See you in a year for the defects." he said cheerfully. It was in the contract that after twelve months the contractor would return with the client and carry out a defects audit. Once these had been rectified, whatever, usually five percent of the contract sum would be released. This was standard practice.

It was now mid-afternoon and Jack had a fair bit of paperwork to catch up on. He thought he might as well do it from home. It seemed pointless to drive past his house and spend at least half an hour to get there depending on the traffic. The car phone rang, a number Jack didn't recognise.

"Jack Watson. How can I help?"

"Hi Jack, it's Brian Rice. I'm on my way over to Epping to discuss your labour requirements."

Bollox Jack thought, that's all I need. Every other day some recruitment agency or other, would check his labour requirements.

"Sorry mate I have left site now and am on the road. I'm about to go into a tunnel so I might lose you."

"Where are you heading?"

Jack disconnected the call and turned his phone off. No matter how many times he told these agencies that he would call them if he needed any additional labour, they kept calling. This really got Jacks back up and at times he found it difficult to keep a civil tongue.

CHAPTER 14

Since Jack joined STG, Julian had been harking on about a big contract that he had tendered for, according to him we were now in the final two. He was convinced we would win the contract. Which was worth nine million. Julian had researched our competitor, and in his opinion, they didn't have the capacity to undertake a job of this size. Neither do STG, thought Jack but he made no comment.

The two companies left in the running for the contract were invited along to give their pitches to ascertain their suitability to be awarded the contract.

As they walked into the foyer of Gladstone Commercial, Jack surveyed his team. Julian wore an ill-fitting light grey suit; his left trouser leg was snagged in his sock and his overgrown white hair was messy. Jack thought he resembled a nutty professor. Steve, was more casual in a blue shirt, opened at the neck and blue trousers. The shoes he wore looked to be three sizes too big and the pointed toes curled up. John, who was there pretending to be a site manager. Apparently, the real ones employed by STG, couldn't be trusted at such an important event. John wore smart jeans and a polo sporting our company logo. Jack thought, we don't have a prayer. They were asked to sit in the waiting area and would be called in shortly.

Julian took the piss out of Steve's shoes. Jack noticed that that this was often the case, not bullying but not far off. Steve, as always shrugged it off. Julian had to dash to the loo.

"Stage fright." Chuckled Steve. When he returned, he had sorted his sock issue but now the tail of his jacket was tucked into his trousers. It was Steves turn to take the piss, Julian didn't enjoy the taste of his own medicine.

The presentation went ok. Jullian waffled on about how great STG are. Then Steve waffled on about the financial stability of the company.
Jack talked through programming. John as usual seemed uninterested and just gave short answers to the questions directed at him. We were thanked for our time and headed for the exit. On the way-out Jack noticed STG's competitors sitting in the waiting area. Three men and a woman, all immaculately dressed in dark suits.
It dawned on Jack that there were no women in senior management at STG. These positions were held by middle aged white men. He often ignored the sexist comments, which were brandished around the office along

with homophobic ones too. There was no racial undertone in the workplace but Jack had yet to meet a person of colour in the offices or on the sites.

Again, Jack was left wondering had he made a mistake taking this role. He pushed this to the back of his mind.

When Julian and Steve got back to their office, they found an irate looking Brian Rice waiting for them.
"Do either of you know where Watson was at three o' clock yesterday?" He asked. They looked at each other blankly and shrugged their shoulders.
"Which one of you is his line manager?"
More blank looks were exchanged.
"Me I suppose." Said Steve.
"Well, you should bloody well know where he was. I phoned him to say I was on my way to site; he told me he was on the road. When I asked where he was going, he hung up and turned his phone off."

"That's not like Jack. I can always get hold of him." Declared Julian.

"Inform Watson I want to have a chat with him after Wednesdays projects review meeting. Don't tell him what it's about." Brian slammed the door as he left. Julian got on the phone to Jack to warn him about Brian. Jack explained that he had never met him and thought he was from an employment agency. Julian laughed,

"Oh no mate he is the construction director and a close personal friend of the managing director." He also warned Jack that Brian had been checking up on him, asking questions.

Jack rattled through his project reviews at the meeting. All positive news including Epping where the client had given him a glowing report. Barry went through the projected final profits, they too all looked good. Julian did his bit on commercial, at one point he cracked a joke. Jack noticed that everyone barring Brian laughed. There was no hiding the animosity between them. As people began leaving the boardroom, Brian said.

"Jack and Steve, can you stay? I'd like a quick word." Surprise surprise thought Jack. When it was just the three of them, Brian began.

"Well Jack how are you settling in with STG?"

"I think it is going quite well."

"Are you getting along with the team?"

"Yes, after some teething problems." Jack lied.

"Barry thinks you are putting a bit too much pressure on him. He says you want everything yesterday." The little shit, Jack thought.

"Brian, the only things I want done yesterday are the things that should have been done yesterday. Have you seen the schedules I have given to him and the buyer?"

"No, can you send me a copy?"

"I have one here." Jack handed it to Brian.

"Very good, you have given plenty of notice. I will have a word with him."

"I am helping Barry with this Brian; we will be up to date by the end of the week," said Steve.

"Ok good, keep me in the loop. Now Jack, would you like to tell us where you were last Thursday afternoon. And why you turned your phone off?"

"Not really, unless you insist?" Brian raised his eyebrow and gestured for him to proceed. Jack explained that it was easier to work from home rather than drive past his house and sit in traffic. He said he didn't turn his phone off.

"Why did you cut me off?" Brian asked firmly.

"Today is the first time I have met you. When you rang me, I thought you were from a recruitment agency. These people are always calling."

"Fair enough. We don't allow working from home. If you're not on site you are to be in the office. Is that clear?"

"As crystal. Perhaps you should be more interested in how well all my projects are going rather than where I am every five minutes."

"It's company policy Jack. Your line manager needs to always know your whereabouts."

"No problem."

"Good man. Let's draw a line under this and move forward." He held out his hand and Jack shook it. On the way-out, Steve asked.

"Are you ok Jack? No one likes a ticking off."

"I'm fine Steve".

"Just be more visible mate, just be more visible.

CHAPTER 15

Jack was wound up for a couple of days after his run-in with Brian. He didn't mention it to Laura as it was best forgotten. After a successful week, Jack checked his emails before shutting down for the weekend. There was one from Brian Rice, which read as follows.

Jack.

This is not an official, or indeed an unofficial warning. I thought it best to record the incident to ensure that it would not be repeated.
The company does not allow working from home. You are expected to work a minimum of forty hours per week as

stated in your contract. You must always be contactable by your line manager and the directors of the company. Your phone should never be switched off during working hours. If you are not on site, you must be in the office. No further action is deemed necessary at this point but any similar occurrences will not be tolerated.

Regards Brian Rice (Construction director).

Jack was furious, not only with the email but for the fact that the M.D. and all the directors were copied in. Julian was not copied in; Brian had been quick to point out he wasn't a board director.

Jack forwarded the email to Julian and asked him to phone to discuss. Ten minutes later he called. Julian thought Brian was out of order sending the email to all. Especially as he shook hands as if the matter was closed. Julian asked Jack "what he was going to do about it, if anything?"

"I don't know, at this moment in time I feel like handing in my notice."

"Don't do anything hasty Jack. The mans a prick, He is not worth losing your job over. Take the weekend to think about it and meet me first thing Monday."

They met at eight o'clock. Jack had decided to stay. Julian was happy and said,

"You won't have to deal with Brian often, just be civil and make sure he sees you around the office."

Jack asked Barry who they used for hiring cranes. They have never used a crane.

"I need one for the roof trusses which are being delivered on Friday."

"I'm not sure how to go about it".

"Do you want me to deal with it Barry."

"That would be great, cheers Jack." He sorted it that morning and told the site manager that he would be on there to supervise the lifts. Maximum six. The mobile crane was on site before eight and the trusses arrived at ten. Jack gave the crane driver the lifting plan and method statement, which he was happy with.

"Nice easy day guv." He said with a smile.

After the third lift, Jack was surprised to see Julian approaching.

"How's it going?"

"All under control boss. What are you doing here? Not checking up on me I hope?"

"No not at all, I am in the area to look at a potential site." Jack knew he was lying and was only too glad that he was going on holiday the following week.

Jack didn't go back to the office that day. Julian phoned him around four o'clock. Jack ignored the call.

CHAPTER 16

Jack aged Seventeen.

Jack was loving every minute of working in the family business. He had developed many skills under Peter's guidance. He was much more advanced than any of his peers at college and his confidence level had never been higher. Jack passed his driving test at the first attempt. Now he could go and pick up materials, this gave Peter a lot more time to work in the garage. After one such collection, Jack shouted.

"Hi Dad, I'm back. I managed to get everything on the list." There was no response which was unusual. He looked in the garage, there was no sign of Peter. He ran into the house. Jo was sitting in her office doing the paperwork.

"Hi mum, where's dad?"

"In the garage love. Where he always is."

"No, he is not there." Jo looked confused.

"He must have popped to the loo, go and have another look. He said he didn't feel great earlier." Jack went back to look for Peter. He wasn't at his bench. Just as he was about to go back to the house, he saw Peter's hand on the floor behind his bench.

"Dad." Peter was unconscious.

"Mum," Jack shouted. "Come quick, Dad has collapsed."

Jo ran in, her face was white with panic. She checked to see if he was breathing, he was. She tried to rouse him by gently shaking his shoulders and calling his name. There was no response.

"What's wrong with him?" Jack cried.

"Jack, calm down, I need you to call an ambulance, now." The paramedics seemed to take forever to arrive, although it was only ten minutes, to Jack it seemed like a lifetime.

The paramedic put an oxygen mask on Peter and injected him with something. He was stable but still unconscious. Jo and Jack went in the ambulance with Peter.

The waiting was the worst part, the not knowing. A young doctor came in and said that Peter was awake and responsive, it was too early to know what had caused him to collapse. He would have to stay in for a few days for tests.

"Can we see him?" Asked Jack.

"Off course, come with me." Peter looked very unwell but tried to put on a brave face for Jo and Jacks sake.

"I'll be home before you know it."

"Do you remember what happened?" asked Jo.

"Yes babe, I dropped my pencil and bent down to pick it up. I got a sharp pain in my head, then I must have passed out. That is all I can remember.

Jo contacted her two sons, Paul and Jim, who both now lived in Scotland. they arrived at the hospital the next day, early in the evening. Jo introduced Jack; this was the first time they had met. The brothers shook his hand almost dismissively and sat down next to their crying mother. Jack sat alone, across from the family group. He said a silent prayer for the best friend he ever had, laying in the hospital bed. He tried hard to convince himself that Peter would be fine and they would be back working in the garage in a couple of days. He thought he better let their clients know that work would be delayed. That's what Peter would do.

After two days of tests, the senior consultant dropped the bombshell to Jo.

"I'm sorry, I have bad news. Peter has a brain tumour."

"What? Can't be. He is as fit as a fiddle."

"I'm afraid the cancer has spread to the rest of his brain, there is nothing we can do."

"No, there must be something, can't you operate?"

The cancer is too advanced, we can only provide palliative care."

"No, no, no." Jo sobbed.

"Not my Peter. How long have we got?"

"Weeks rather than months," said the sullen looking consultant. Jo screamed and fell to the floor sobbing and crying out.

"Not my Peter, not my Peter. Please God not my Peter." Paul and Jim did their best to comfort Jo. Jack sat alone in disbelief.

Jack never got the chance to say a proper goodbye. Peter fell into a coma on the same day the consultant broke the news.

Three weeks after he collapsed Peter passed away peacefully. All four were at his bedside when the monitor flatlined. Jack wept quietly and asked himself why? It all seemed so unfair. What would happen to him now?
Jim said.
"What are you crying for? He's not your fucking dad".
"That's a cruel thing to say Jim, apologise now." Jo insisted."
Jack didn't wait for an apology he ran out of the room crying loudly. Jo lowered her head, still sobbing and kissed her beloved husband on the forehead and whispered.
"Wait for me darling, I will join you one day."

The funeral was a small affair. Jo had decided to sell the house and close the business. It was too much for her to stay, too many memories. She planned to move to Scotland and live with Jim. Jack was devastated and at the wake he found Jim alone in the kitchen.

"What the fuck do you want? Asked a drunk sounding Jim. Jack didn't reply. He picked up a saucepan and smashed it into Jim's face. He was knocked out cold. Jack went back to the front room where the guests were chatting quietly. He went up to Jo, kissed her firmly on the cheek and hugged her tight.

"Goodbye mum, thanks for everything you and dad have done for me." He kissed her again. And walked away.

"Where are you going son?" Jack didn't turn around. This was the last time he saw Jo.

CHAPTER 17

Now.

Jack and Laura had a lovely holiday with little Robbie in the Spanish sunshine. Deep-down, Laura knew Jack wasn't quite himself. He appeared to be distracted, distant at times. He never brought his work home but recently Jack was doing stuff on Saturdays and sometimes Sundays. This wasn't like him; she knew something was troubling her handsome man.

On the third night, when Robbie was away in the land of dreams, she decided she had to broach the subject.

"Darling is everything all right? You seem a little quieter than usual."

"No, my love, I'm fine, just a little tired."

"You know you can tell me Jack, we agreed, no secrets. I know you babe. Is it something at work?"

"It's nothing to worry your pretty little head about Laura. There are a couple of pricks annoying me but I can handle them." Jack went on to talk about his run-ins with Barry and how John was a pain in the arse, with his persistent singing of the twelve days of Christmas. He didn't mention the major issue with Brian. He was slipping back into his old ways of bottling things up. Jack knew this was wrong but he thought he could sort it out quickly. Laura didn't sleep well that night, why was he not telling her the whole story? She tried not to let it worry her but that was easier said than done.

Jack arrived bright and early at the Potters bar office on his return from his holiday. The young girl on reception, Karen, complimented him on his tan, saying how jealous she was. When he got upstairs, he was surprised to see Julian at his desk.

"Morning Julian, how's it going? Did you miss me?"

"Come in Jack. Close the door and sit down."

Shit, Jack had forgotten about not answering his phone on the last day before his break.

"Why did you ignore my calls Jack?"

"I'm sorry Julian I was so angry over that email from Brian that I didn't want to talk to anyone."

"For fucks sake, you haven't got an abundance of allies, just me and Steve."

"I know mate. It was wrong. All I can do is apologise."

"I didn't mention it to Brian, if I had, you would be out the door."

"I appreciate it Julian, thanks."

"Please don't let it happen again Jack."

"Aye, Aye captain." Jack saluted. Julian went on to add that the company had leased two units in an industrial park just a five-minute walk from where they sat. He explained that all the team involved in the new build side of the business would move there the following week.

"Including my nemesis?" Jack asked.

"Yes, Brian too, but he will be in the other office to ours."

"Well let's be grateful for small mercies." Jack laughed. Julian gave a wry smile and shook his head.

"Come on, let me show you our new home." During the short walk, Julian asked about Jacks holiday. It was like he had forgotten the attempted rollocking he delivered only minutes earlier. Jack liked this say your piece and move on attitude.

The new offices were on the third floor. The building was security conscious with a fob entry system, and coded entry on each level. There was a designated parking area for each company. Jack was impressed by the size of the space. In the main area was a series of eight desks butted up to each other. All had Pc's and telephones. There were two further desks in the corners either side of the door. A glass partition separated the main area from a smaller side office which was where Julian and Steve would be. Jack thought, great now I will be able to see them when they play their shoot the squirrel game.

"Pick a desk Jack, you can have first choice."

"Sweet, I'll have this one by the door. It will be better for the office-based team to sit together." Julian agreed.

"Before you go Jack, we have switched site manager while you were away. Alan, who you haven't met is now at Luton. You will need to keep an eye on him as he tends to cock things up."

"Is he new?"

"No, he has been with the company for years, almost part of the furniture. He has only been a site manager for a short time."

"Why don't they get rid of him if he is no good?"

"He is dependable and trustworthy; he just needs a little guidance."

When jack arrived at Luton, the site seemed quiet. From outside he could see the brickwork was completed. This surprised and pleased him as it wasn't due to finish until the following week. He walked into the site office and Alan jumped.

"Jesus, you frightened the life out of me." Jack introduced himself. Alan was a little bloke whose face bore the signs of many winters spent outside. he looked to be in his sixties. He told Jack that there was no operatives on site as the roofer wasn't due yet.

"Did you call him, to see if he could start earlier?"

"No, I was told to keep to the program, and not change things."

"Ok, I will give him a call later. Let's have a walk around the site." Jack noticed quite a few issues which he pointed out needed addressing. Alan took notes. One was quite serious. The bricklayers had installed old concrete blocks as padstones for the steel beams to support the roof. Jack told Alan to order the ones specified by the engineer and get them changed.

"But that's how we always do it." Alan protested.

"For fuck sakes, If I here that's how we always do it one more time I will lose the plot. Get them changed Alan, before building control see them."

"Ok boss, consider it done." Alan looked like a chastised child. The site in Hemel was also ahead of schedule and was being run much better than Luton. Jack didn't have to micromanage George. He was able to spend the rest of the day back in his office going through his paperwork and updating his reports. He read an email from admin which made him smile. He was in fourth place in the football tipping competition, just Two points behind the leader. There were eight games left so he was in with a chance. An even bigger smile came to his face when he saw who was bottom, Brian Rice.

CHAPTER 18

Over the next few weeks, Jack was predominantly at his desk in the fancy new office. Brian was a frequent visitor, popping his shaven head in two or three times a day. Always making a point of smiling in Jacks direction. Almost as if he had gained a major victory.

Julian had asked Jack to produce a programme to build a block of thirty-five flats. The STG surveyor's would then submit a tender for the contract. Julian had suggested a duration of around forty-five weeks would be competitive. Jack didn't like this, as it was his job to determine durations of contracts. Jack was finding it increasingly difficult to concentrate with all the small talk and attempts at humour sounding out around the office. He walked out when John sang about that fucking partridge. After a short walk to get some fresh air, he went in to see Brian.

"Can I have a word Brian?"

"Sure, shoot." Brian replied looking a bit concerned.

"I can't concentrate next door, there is constant noise and distraction. I am used to working in a quieter environment."

"Come on Jack, it can't be that bad?"

"Have you heard what it's like when John starts singing his Christmas carols and everyone laughs?"

"Just tell him to shut up."

"Yeah, like he will listen to me. Can I have permission to complete this program from home? I don't want to get it wrong."

"No Jack. I have told you the company policy on working from home. It is not allowed."

Jack walked out shaking his head.

"I'll have a word with them." Brian called out.

"Please don't, that will only make matters worse."

Jack worked on his program all over the weekend before it was due. Explaining to Laura the importance of getting it right. She wasn't happy and knew her handsome man was struggling. She was hurting because he didn't confide in her like he always had in the past.

Jack presented Julian with the contract.

"Do we really need fifty weeks Jack?"

"Yes Jullian, why else would I have put it?"

"This could cost us the contract."

"Tell the surveyor's forty-five weeks if you want, but don't put my name to it."

"Ok Fifty it is."

Jack went back to his desk. He saw Brian, chatting and laughing with John. Brenda, from admin walked in with a big smile on her face and headed straight for Jack.

"Congratulations to our champion." The room went silent. She handed Jack an envelope which had one hundred and seventy pounds written on it. He was so busy over the weekend that he had completely forgotten about the football. "Looks like he won." Barry broke the silence.

"I Can't believe it; he has only been here five minutes and he has the cheek to win first prize."

He said with an attempt at humour. Jack opened the envelope and took the cash out. He splayed it into a fan shape and stood up.

"It looks like construction is not the only thing I know more about than you lot." He said waving the cash in the air. This went down like a lead balloon. Brian stormed out; the others focused on their work. The silence was deafening. If only it could be like this all the time Jack thought. He was oblivious to how much he had alienated himself with his comment. Julian was stood at his desk with his palms out. With an exasperated look and a shrug of his shoulders he turned away.

On his way home, Jacks phone rang.
"Hi Julian, what can I do for you?"
"Do you do it on purpose Jack or are you just stupid?"
"What are you on about man?"
"When you left, your ears must have been ringing from the torrent of abuse aimed at you. It is safe to say you are the most unpopular bloke in this office by a country mile. Even Steve has turned against you."
"None of them had the balls to say anything to my face."
"Just watch your back Jack, the knives are being sharpened. See you tomorrow."
"Bye Julian."

Jack was fuming but managed to hide it when he got home.

CHAPTER 19

Jack aged nineteen.

Jack sat quietly in the waiting area outside court number two at Snaresbrook crown court. His case was due to be heard next. The charge was grievous bodily harm on a police constable. Jack had entered a plea of not guilty. The co-defendant, his friend Paul had changed to a guilty plea at the last minute. Sitting with Jack was Julie, His barrister. An attractive woman in her early forties. Even in her court wig, jack thought she looked hot. She tried to convince him to plead guilty as the evidence was damning. She highlighted his options. If Jack pleaded not guilty and was convicted, as seemed likely. He would receive a prison sentence of between five and seven years. On the other hand, if he pleaded guilty, because of his age he would get sent to borstal for a period of between six months to two years. Most offenders were released in under a year with good behaviour.

Jack's mind flashed back to the night of the incident. He was having a good night out with Paul, who he had met a few months earlier. A fight broke out over some girl and spilled over onto the street. The police were on the scene in no time, only two of them, both in their fifties. One of them grabbed jack while the other was trying to control the rest of the raging mob. Paul smashed his forearm into the back of the head of the PC holding Jack. He fell to the floor. The two of them rained kicks on the injured constable. Running off leaving him unconscious on the ground.

The PC was in hospital with severe damage to his vertebrae. He identified Paul Adams as one of the assailants but didn't know the identity of the other.

Both Paul and Jack, were arrested on the same evening at different locations. Apparently, Paul had a photograph of both Jack and him in his wallet. The injured PC identified Jack as the other assailant.

"Jack, this is your last chance to change your plea. Trust me you will be found guilty. Please make this easier on yourself."
Jack reluctantly agreed. The jury were dismissed. The judge asked were there any mitigating circumstances before he passed sentence. Julie went over Jacks troubled childhood and his spell in and out of foster care. She highlighted how he was left devastated and alone after the death of his foster parent Peter. A man he loved so much he called dad. She said Jack was sorry beyond words

for his actions and had agreed to counselling.

Jack and Paul, both got the same sentence as forecast by Julie. Six months to two years at a borstal in Kent.

CHAPTER 20

Now.

A few weeks after jack won the money, he was still being treated like a bit of an outcast. Colleagues barely saying hello or good morning. Conversations with all the team were only work related. This office environment suited Jack better, at least now he could focus on his work in the near silent atmosphere that existed whenever he was around. He knew well that all changed when he wasn't around. Fuck them he thought. He got along with the site managers and all the sub-contractors which was the most important thing and the projects continued to run smoothly.

Jack's six-month appraisal was due. He walked into the boardroom five minutes early. Already seated were Brian and Steve. Julian was conspicuous by his absence.

"Take a seat Jack, this shouldn't take long." Steve said gesturing to a chair opposite from them. Brian ran through the elements of the appraisal; Jack was surprised he scored highly in all the elements apart from working as part of a team. Steve added that Jack's ability and knowledge were a great asset and both clients and contractors spoke very highly of him. Then he added.

"You have got to be more of a team player mate."

"Believe me, I have tried Steve."

Brian jumped in.

"Come on, let's be honest here. You see yourself as better than the rest of your team."

"Brian, if we are being honest, cards on the table and all that jazz. Let me tell you how it is from my viewpoint as all you have, are the grumblings of others."

"Yes, please continue, the floor is yours."

"Ok Barry first. Everything I have suggested has been met with resistance. I must fight for every change to the way things have been done in the past. When he doesn't like it, he goes bitching to you." Brian didn't look up from the notes he was busily taking. For all Jack knew he could have been writing gibberish. Steve remained quiet.

"Carry on Jack."

"John has never listened to me, he does what he likes when he likes, I don't think he answers to anyone. Julian. He talks a lot of nonsense, often repeating the same old stories." Jack paused for a sip of water.

"Have you got a good word to say about anyone?" Steve asked with eyebrows raised.

"Not really. Steve, you try to please everyone. You spend so much time sitting on the fence your arse must be full of splinters."

"Careful Jack don't overstep the mark." said a serious looking Brian.

"But you said, let's be honest. So, I am. It's nothing personal."

"Anything else?" Jack was on a roll, there was no stopping him. He was clearly enjoying himself.

"Just you Brian. From the day I hung up on you."

"So, at last you admit that you did hang up on me?"

"I said at the time that I did. What I denied was turning my phone off. You only hear what you want to hear. Anyway, from that day you have being trying to get rid of me."

"That's not true."

"Yes it is. The trouble is I'm good at my job, never late and never have a day off. So, you have tried to make my work life as unbearable as you can, in the hope that I will quit."

"That's rubbish." Shouted Brian, his face reddening.

111

"I thought we were being honest. I have investigated constructive dismissal so good luck with the path you have chosen."

"You really do think you're a smart arse don't you Jack?" Brian was now completely red faced and looking at Steve for support.

"I don't think it. The thing is I'm smarter than you Brian, deal with it. I will leave STG when I choose too, on my terms, are we done gentleman?" Both Steve and Brian sat in silence as Jack left the boardroom.

Jack was proud of himself, the way he stood up to the bullying Brian. He didn't share the experience with Laura, she would only worry.

For the next two weeks, Jack worked from site. George was on annual leave, a nice trip to Malta where his daughter was getting married. Jack considered using an agency site manager but the project was going so well he didn't want it to fall back. Plus, he had the bonus of not going to the office each day. The atmosphere there now was positively frosty. On the second day at Hemel, Jack got a visit from Julian.

"Don't tell me you were just in the area so you thought you would pop in?"

"Don't start your bollox with me Jack, Brian wants you watched like a hawk. One slip and he will be all over you like a rash."

"Sorry Julian, thanks for the warning mate."

"You never heard it from me Jack, if he finds out I tipped you off, I too will be in the shit."

"No worries mate."

"What are your plans Jack? Are you staying with STG?"

I haven't decided yet, you will be the first to know when I have."

"Fair enough. Right, I better head back and report to Hitler." Julian said with a wave and a smile.

Over the course of the next two weeks Jack was treated to all kinds of surprise visitors from the office who just happened to be passing through. On a couple of occasions, he saw Brian Rice's car parked at the end of the road. He was too much of a coward to show his face.

Laura noticed a big change in Jack while he was babysitting the site in Hemel. She had her husband back. Every evening, he came home with a big smile and played with young Robbie until his bedtime. Then they'd snuggle up and watch a film, just like the old days. Laura longed for this to be the norm as before.

They chatted about how happy Jack was being on site, not cooped up in an office. Laura told him if he wanted to leave STG and go back into site management, she would back him all the way. Jack laughed.

"You know it will be less money darling?"

"But more happiness, my handsome man."

CHAPTER 21

Jack aged eighteen.

Jack spent ten months locked up in borstal. He would have got out sooner but for a bit of bother in the first month. He shared a cell with a mix raced fella. Carl, he was in for stealing cars. and had been there for six months so he knew the ropes. He explained the gang culture in the borstal. There were three main groups, the whites, the blacks and the Muslims. You can choose to hook up with the white boys or you can be a free spirit like me. But rest assured Jack, you will be approached very soon. You will be promised protection, which of course comes at a price, usually cigarettes or tobacco. Jack only smoked weed on the outside. If you turn them down then one of the other gangs will try to make you, their bitch. It's not easy Jack, you either run with the gang, which will mean attacking me to show your loyalty, or you stand alone.

"Fuck that, I'm no racist. Let them try their shit on me."

"Be careful my man. They will come."

Jack thanked Carl for the advice.

He didn't have to wait long. On the second afternoon three big blokes came into Jacks cell.

"You get out." one of them said as he grabbed Carl by the scruff of the neck and marched him to the door.

"Leave him alone." Jack protested.

"Sit down and shut up arsehole." said the smallest of the three. The biggest stood at the door keeping a look out for screws.

I'm Stan, also known as switch. I run things around here. For a small fee I will make sure no one bothers you while your in."

"No thanks, I can take care of myself." Jack replied as confidently as he could, he was aware his voice was shaky."

"You're not listening dickhead, it's not negotiable".

Jack lunged headfirst at Stan, before he got to his target, he felt a crushing blow to the back of his neck. Jack was battered for what seemed like an age, although it lasted only around thirty seconds. As he lay curled up on the floor, he heard a voice.

"Get up Watson." Jack turned his head to see warden Jones hovering over him. "Not so handsome now, are you Cop beater?" Jack groaned as he got to his feet.

"Who did this to you?"

"I fell over."

"I fell over sir," Jones snarled and kicked Jack in the shin.

"I fell over sir." Jack repeated.

"Not a good start Watson, I'll have to put you on report."

"Yes sir."

Jack's punishment was two weeks loss of privileges. This meant he had no recreation time and wasn't allowed to go out to the exercise yard. But the biggest blow was that he had no hope of getting out in six months. Because he kept his mouth shut, Jack had gained some respect and was left alone by all the gangs.

Jack signed up for the woodwork classes and it wasn't long before the tutor Mr Kayle, A retired joiner, spotted his ability with wood.

"You're a natural son." Jack liked the way he called him son. But it didn't resonate quite the same as when Peter said it.

"My stepdad taught me from an early age."

"Well lad he must be disappointed that you have ended up in here?"

"He would be if he was still alive sir."

"Sorry Jack"

"Don't worry about it Mr Kayle, how where you to know?"

Jack liked his tutor very much; he was old school and taught in the same manner as Peter had and he also had the same scent of wood about him.

Mr Kayle got Jack to help with the classes and he was only too pleased to pass on the skills he had learnt at the hands of his best mate Peter.

Jack was popular with the class and showed them all kinds of woodworking skills. Teaching how to make strong joints was his favourite, from the simple half lap to mortice and tenon and finally on to the intricate but best looking of all joints, the dovetail.

Mr Kayle had got Jack a position as a joiner for a company based in Hackney, East London. Jack was delighted and couldn't thank him enough.

"You have a God given talent son, don't throw it away. Keep your nose clean and you will be very successful."

"Thanks Mr Kyle."

Part of Jack's terms for early release was that he had to continue with his counselling once a week for the following fourteen months. Jack thought that was a small price to pay for his freedom.

CHAPTER 22

Now.

Jack, decided to take a grievance out against Brian Rice. Citing all the incidents since he accused Jack of turning off his phone, which of course he did but vehemently denied. His statement read that he believed that by his actions, Brian was trying to force him to resign. Jack was convinced Brian had encourage the members of the team to make life difficult for him. Jack also resented the fact that Brian was continually sending scouts to keep track of Jack's every move, just waiting for him to slip up. Which of course he never did.

The MD Adam got wind of this and was far from happy. He called an immediate board meeting to address this situation. Present around the circular board room table were, Steve Gin, Jack's line manager, who as always shifted uncomfortably in his seat, he hated confrontation. Richard Greening, the senior surveyor. He didn't have any day-to-day dealings with Jack. He was there to discuss the financial impact Jack had made at STG. Brian sat opposite Adam. He also looked ill at ease.

"Right." Said Adam, who would chair the meeting.

"Brian, would you like to respond to the allegations made by Jack Watson?"

"I must say I was very surprised when I got the memo. I think the bloke is being paranoid."

"So, you haven't been hounding him, sending people to check his whereabouts, Asking questions?"

"To a degree, But Adam, you saw the warning email I sent shortly after Watson started. It's my job to keep an eye on him."

"We all felt that email was unnecessary and you overreacted. You made it personal Brian. It's clear you don't like him the way you refer to him by his surname".

"That wasn't my intention, I can't believe I'm on trial here."

"There you go again, overreacting." Adam was getting annoyed.

"Steve, how do you feel Jack is doing?" Mr fence sitter looked nervous but at least he spoke the truth. Much to Brian's annoyance.

"He has great knowledge for a man of his age and his planning and programming are second to none. He makes the tasks of the other team members simple and straight forward."

"So why the animosity towards Jack?"

"He is a bit of a lone wolf. He wants things done his way and to his time scales. I don't think the others like that."

"Isn't that why we gave him the job?"

"Yes Adam. Perhaps it's just a clash of personalities?"

"Or other contract managers have been too soft." Brian was now raging inside. The MD was backing Watson.

"Richard, from a financial viewpoint, how are the projects that Jack is overseeing looking?"

"Great Adam. Projected profits are up five percent since Jack took the reins."

"So, to be clear. Jack Watson is good at his job and dependable?" Steve nodded while Brian shrugged his shoulders.

"For god's sake Brian, grow up. Your personal dislike of someone isn't grounds for a witch hunt. This stops here and now. Have I made myself clear?"

"Yes Adam. Crystal."

"If Jack leaves, we will lose an asset and I will hold you personally responsible Brian. Make this situation go away."

"Ok Adam." The meeting was over. Brian walked out without a word to anyone, He looked like a scalded child. Steve didn't say anything but he loved watching the bully squirm.

"Steve, I want you to have a word with Jack, off the record. Tell him about this meeting and how he has my backing."

"I'm sure he will be happy and relieved to hear that Adam."

Later that afternoon, Steve passed on the news to jack. He couldn't keep the broad grin from his face.

"Still watch your back, he has many eyes and ears."

"Is this still off the record Steve?"

"Yes mate."

"Then fuck him."

CHAPTER 23

After the board meeting, Jack felt more assured. He was strutting around the office like a proud peacock. He knew that everyone by now had heard that the MD was a fan of his. There was still no small talk about football or what show was popular on television, not when Jack was around anyway. It didn't bother him in the slightest, he despised them more than they disliked him.

The projects in Hemel and Luton were both nearing completion, and both were ahead of program. More brownie points for Jack. He approached Steve to ask what was on the agenda after these two were finished. Steve waffled on about what might be coming up if our bids were successful. He informed Jack that they had lost the next contract with Epping, due to the farce over the asbestos problem. Jack was gutted to hear this as Epping was right on his doorstep, a lovely commute.

The only project that was about to come live was in Croydon, South London. Alarm bells rang for Jack. That would be a nightmare of a journey. Steve handed Jack a file containing the specification and contract drawings.

"Get your head around that, sunshine. Can you get a revised program and procurement schedule over to me by the end of next week?" Jack feigned interest.

"Ok Steve, no problem mate." They often called each other mate. Nothing could have been further from the truth.

Jack and Laura received an invitation to a fiftieth birthday party, from one of

Jack's former directors. It was to be held the following weekend in Liverpool Street.

"What do you think Jack, do you want to go?"

"Yes babe, why not? I left on good terms and a night out will do us both the world of good, and it's a freebie, so the booze will taste even sweeter."

Laura laughed.

"You're some cookie Mr Watson."

It was lovely to catch up with his old colleagues. Jack thought his wife looked beautiful in her figure-hugging green dress which seemed to really highlight her hair, and he told her so.

"You don't look to shabby yourself."

Laura said, blushing slightly. Jack noticed but chose not to mention it. Boy did he love this woman.

Later in the evening the chat turned to how Jack was getting on in his new role. He said it was up and down and he wasn't enjoying the office-based side of the position.

"You are welcome to come back." said Jack's former MD. Mike. Jack thanked him. He noticed Laura was smiling at the invite.

"Thanks again Mike. I'll bare it in mind."

The rest of the evening was a blast. It had been years since Jack and Laura had danced so much together. By the end of the night, they only had eyes for each other. They awoke the next morning with happy hangovers.

"Would you go back darling?"

"Sure, why not? It's nice to have that option. I'll stick where I am for now. I think a have turned a corner."

"Ok my handsome man, you know I will support you whatever you choose." Jack kissed her and they snuggled up for another doze. The little man was still asleep.

CHAPTER 24

Jack aged twenty- two.

Jack, once again found himself sitting outside a courtroom, waiting for his case to be heard. This time it was court 13 at Wood Green crown court in North London. He was charged with three offences. Actual bodily harm, resisting arrest and assault on a police officer. Jack had pleaded not guilty on all three counts against him. After lengthy discussions with his barrister, this would change once Jack was in the dock.

Judge Prior would preside on the case. Jack was told to stand, as the charges were read out.

The clerk of the court. "Can you confirm your name and address for the court?" Jack confirmed.

"Do you understand the charges brought against you?"

"Yes."

"On count one, causing actual bodily harm to Mr J Williams. Do you plead guilty, or not guilty?"

"Guilty." There were mumbles from the public gallery. No one looked more surprised than Mr William's family. A few high fives were exchanged.

"On count two, resisting arrest. How do you plead, guilty, or not guilty?"

"Guilty."

"On count three, assault on a police officer. How do you plead, guilty, or not guilty?"

"Not guilty."

Judge Prior, explained to the jury that there would only be one charge that they would be called Upon to consider, which was count three, Assault on a police officer. All the witnesses, who had been called to give evidence on the first two counts, were thanked and excused. The judge, then called for a recess until the following morning, to allow both the prosecution, Mr Ralph Stone. and the defence, Mr Cyril Baker, time to prepare for the one charge against Mr Watson.

Court resumed at nine thirty. Judge Prior, asked for the opening statements from both prosecution and defence. Once the arguments had been outlined. The prosecution called their first witness. PC Grey. The alleged victim. After been sworn in by the clerk, proceedings began.

Mr Stone. "In your own words, can you describe the events of the evening of the twenty third of August this year?"

PC Grey. "Yes, my colleague, PC Archer and I responded to a radio call of a disturbance outside the Manor House Public house."

Mr Stone. "Can you describe the scene when you got there?"

PC Grey. "There was a fight between at least two people, one male was on the ground, another was on top aiming punches and kicks. A large crowd had gathered."

Mr Stone. "What action did you take?"

PC Grey. "The crowd dispersed a little when they heard the sirens. I ran over and knocked the attacker off the prone victim."

Mr Stone. "Is the attacker, as you call him, in the court today?"

PC Grey. "Yes, he is the defendant."

Mr Stone. "Then what happened?"

PC Grey. "I managed to restrain the assailant. He was struggling, trying to break free from my grip. I had just managed to get my handcuffs out when something hit my squad car, as I jumped, the assailant swung his elbow into my face, I fell to the ground. The assailant ran off to cheers from the crowd."

Mr Stone. "So, you are saying that the defendant, Mr Jack Watson, deliberately elbowed you in the face, to make his escape?"

PC Grey. "That is correct. I sustained a bloody nose in the attack, but nothing was broken".

Mr Stone. "Then what happened?"

PC Grey. "More officers had arrived at the scene; they soon had the defendant under arrest. He was charged with the three counts you heard read out to the court yesterday."

Mr Stone. "Thank you PC Grey, no further questions."
Judge Prior. "Does the defence have any questions?"

Mr Baker. "Just a few your Honour. PC Grey, were there any witnesses to the alleged assault on you by my client?"

PC Grey. "Not as such, my colleague saw the scuffle."

MR Baker." So no, is the answer to my question?"

PC Grey. No, but I bloody felt it."

Judge Prior. "Stick to answering the questions constable."

PC Grey. "Sorry your honour."

Mr Baker. "I put it to you constable, that when you were distracted by the noise of something hitting the patrol car. The defendant pulled his arm away from you sharply, causing you to fall to the ground."

PC Grey. "No, he struck me with his elbow."

Mr Baker. "Come on constable, it's clear what happened. You dropped your guard and the defendant got away. You concocted this assault to save you from embarrassment. Is that not what happened constable?"

PC Grey. No, that man assaulted me." He said pointing to Jack Watson, who sat stone faced in the dock.

Mr Baker. "No further questions your honour."

Judge Prior. "The prosecution can call their next witness." PC Bennet was sworn in.

Mr Stone. "You were with PC Grey on the night in question?"

PC Bennet. "Yes sir, that is correct."

Mr Stone. "Tell the jury in your own words, what you saw happen."

PC Bennet. "I was calming the crowd down and trying to clear the area. I saw PC Grey was having difficulty restraining one of the men involved in the fight."

Mr Stone. "What did you do then?"

PC Bennet. "I ran over to assist my colleague. The person being detained was trying to get away, his free arm was swinging wildly. Then I saw a shopping trolley hit the patrol car. When I looked back, I saw the detainee had got away. Another officer was in hot pursuit."

Mr Stone. "No further questions your honour."

The defence council got to his feet and approached the witness box.

Mr Baker. "Did you see the defendant elbow constable Grey in the face?"

PC Bennet. "No."

Mr Baker. "No further questions your honour."

The prosecution's final witness was the arresting officer. He also testified that he hadn't seen the defendant strike PC Grey. Court was adjourned for the day. The case for the defence would be heard in the morning.

CHAPTER 25

Because he knew the policeman would lie in court, Jack couldn't risk a long prison sentence. Given his previous conviction. He got a friend of his, a mini cab driver to testify as a witness, even though he wasn't at the scene of the incident. Jack's reasoning was if they were prepared to lie, It was the only hope he had.

Mr Baker, called the first witness for the defence.

Mr Baker. "Please state your name and occupation for the court."

"John Ramsey, mini cab driver."

Mr Baker. "Tell me John, I can call you John?" The witness nodded.

"Where you working in the Manor House area on the evening of August twenty third, this year?"

John. "Yes sir, I was."

Mr Baker. "Did you see an altercation outside the Manor House, Public house?"

John. "Yes sir, I did. The traffic had been stopped by several police cars parked randomly in the road."

Mr Baker. "Did you see the defendant being detained by the police?"

John. Yes sir, I did. It was hysterical."

Mr Baker. "What do you mean by hysterical John?"

John. "Well sir, the policeman had hold of the defendants arm. A shopping trolley was thrown from the crowd, hitting the police car. The defendant yanked his arm free, and the policeman ended up on his arse. It reminded me of the game I play with my daughter. She grips my hand as tight as she can. I pull away and she falls onto the bed. The policeman went down the same way." The public gallery laughed at this analogy and it also brought a smile to a few of the jurors faces. Jack saw this as a positive.

Mr Baker. "So, to be clear, the defendant was facing the police constable, when he made a run for it?"

John. "That is correct sir."

Mr Baker. "No further questions your honour."

Judge Prior. Does the prosecution have any questions?"

Mr Stone. "Yes your honour." He approached the witness box.

"John, can you tell the jury how long you have been friends with the defendant?" A gasp could be heard from the public gallery. Jack remained emotionless.

John. "I have never met the defendant."

Mr Stone. "Come on John, you don't expect us to believe that Do you?"

John. "You can believe what you like, It's the truth."

Mr Stone. "So, you expect us to believe that you're a law-abiding citizen just doing his duty?"

John. "I was asked to come to court to give evidence about what I saw."

Mr Stone. "Don't you think it unusual, that out of all of the crowd gathered, you were the only witness to the event in question?"

Mr Baker. "Objection your honour, He is asking the witness to comment on what others saw."

Judge Prior. "Sustained."

Mr Stone. "You are prepared to give up three days' work to help a complete stranger?"

John. "I work nights." The court erupted with laughter. Jack refrained but was laughing inside.

Mr Stone. "You have had your fair share of run inns with the police John, is that true to say?"

Mr Baker. "Objection your honour. The witnesses past has no bearing on what he saw."

Judge Prior. "Overruled. Tread carefully Mr Stone. You may answer the question." The judge looked in the direction of the witness.

John. "Yes, I had a few minor incidents when I was young. Nothing serious."

Mr Stone. "How old were you when you had, as you put it, your last minor incident?"

John. "Thirty." More laughs erupted from the gallery, much to judge Prior's disapproval. He banged his gavel and called for order.

Mr Stones. "Hardly young John. No further questions your honour." The judge called for a recess, as it was nearing lunchtime. Jack thought that John's evidence was neither good nor bad. It was all he had. Jack was on next; This didn't stop him enjoying his burger and fries at McDonalds.

The court reconvened at two o'clock. Jack took the stand and was sworn in.

Mr Baker. Jack, can you explain to the jury, why you have pleaded guilty to two of the three charges brought against you and not the third?"

Jack." I was involved in a fight, which ended with my opponent needing hospital treatment. So, I am guilty as charged. I tried to make a run for it, so also guilty on resisting arrest. But I did not assault a police officer, no matter what he testified."

Mr Baker. "Tell the jury about your arrest."

Jack. "I was on top of this guy who had been looking for trouble all evening. That's not an excuse for my actions. I had a bit to drink and got carried away. I heard the sirens and was about to run away, when a policeman knocked me off my opponent."

Mr Baker. "Were you facing each other Jack? Think, this is important."

Jack. "Yes, the whole time. He had hold of my arm and was trying to get his handcuffs out. I admit I was trying to get away. I heard a crashing noise. This caused the policeman to look the other way. He was distracted, I saw my chance. A sharp pull of my arm and I ran off."

Mr Baker. "Did you elbow PC Grey in the face?"

Jack. "No."

Mr Baker. "Did you strike, or attempt to strike PC Grey?"

Jack. "No."

Mr Baker. "What happened when you ran off?"

Jack. "As I said I had a few to drink. As I was running, I managed to trip over my own feet and landed face first on the ground. Another policeman pinned me down, cuffed and arrested me."

Mr Baker. "Thank you, Jack. No further questions. The defence council was on his feet in a flash.

Mr Stone. "Tell the court about your relationship with John."

Jack. "I don't know him."

Mr Stone. "So, you expect us to believe, out of thirty plus people at the scene, only one good citizen came forward?"

Jack. "It looks that way."

Mr Stone. "How very convenient. Do you like hitting policeman Jack?"

Mr Baker. "Objection, your honour. Unreasonable line of questioning."

Judge Prior. "Sustained."

Mr Stone. "Have you, like John had many run inns with the police?"

Mr Baker. "Objection, your honour. Irrelevant.

Judge Prior, "Sustained. You are on very thin ice councillor."

Mr Stones. "I put it to you that you knew you were in serious trouble. Assault on a police officer is severely frowned upon. That is why you concocted John's testimony. I doubt he was even there."

Jack. "I didn't hit the officer."

Mr Stones. "I don't believe you Jack. I would be very surprised if the jury do either. No further questions your honour."

Judge Prior. "Members of the jury, it has been a long day. The court is in recess until ten am tomorrow. We will hear the summing up from both parties then. Do not discuss this case with anyone, apart from fellow members of the jury."

Jack was on his way home when his phone rang. The number was vaguely familiar.

"Hello?"

"Hello, my old mucker, how did I do? I played a fucking blinder, right."

"Hi John. You sure did, the lord himself would have believed your shite." John laughed.

"You can buy me a couple of pints when I see you next."

"No problem. It could take a while. The old bill could keep an eye on my movements. I'll find out after the verdict in the morning."

"Your innocent mate. A blind man could see it. You will be as free as a bird, trust me."

"Thanks for your positivity John."

"That's alright, listen, do you want me to come along in the morning for a bit of morale support?"

"Are you a fucking retard John?"

"What?"

"We don't know each other, Remember?"

"Oh yeah. Sorry, forgot that bit. Good luck anyway, Toodle pip." John hung up before Jack could reply.

CHAPTER 26

Mr Stones stood close to the jury, as he began the summing up for the prosecution. Jack thought, he had a similar demeanour to the fictional TV lawyer, Perry Mason.

"Ladies and gentlemen of the jury. PC Grey, an officer who has served you, the public for over eight years, has told you that the defendant assaulted him. Ask yourselves, why would he lie? Don't be fooled by the fact that the defendant pleaded guilty to the two lesser crimes for which he was charged. This is a very clever tactic, no doubt instigated by my learned friend for the defence. Don't think for a moment that because he admitted those charges, that he didn't commit the third and most serious. Assault on a police officer. And what do we make of the only witness, who claims to have seen the whole incident, while sitting in traffic. A man who claims, not to have known the defendant. Pull the other one it's got bells on it. A thirty strong crowd had gathered at the scene of the fight; plus, however many cars were stuck in traffic. Yet John Ramsey, a man known to police, is the only one to come forward. PC Grey's version of events are the only true facts here. He was trying to arrest the defendant and was knocked to the ground, courtesy of the defendants elbow. Causing a bloody nose and two black eyes. PC Grey needed medical treatment from a paramedic. The defendant himself, admitted that he got carried away while he was fighting. I put it to you, that he also got carried away when PC Grey tried to arrest him. Who are we to believe? The words of John Ramsey, a lifelong petty criminal or, those of a serving police officer. A man whose sole duty is to uphold the law and protect people such as you and I. There is no doubt in my mind that the defendant is guilty as charged, and I'm confident that you will return a guilty verdict. Thank you, ladies and gentlemen of the jury."

In Jack's view. Mr. Baker's demeanour was akin to Rumpole of the bailey, another fictional TV barrister. His voice was strikingly similar.

Mr Baker. "Ladies and gentlemen of the jury. There can only be one verdict you can return, based on the little evidence we have to go on. Not Guilty. The defendant and the defence's only witness, give the same account of events. The prosecution only have the words of an embarrassed police constable. PC Grey, let go of the defendant, due to the distraction of the shopping trolley hitting the patrol car.

The defendant pulled himself clear and PC Grey fell to the ground. The only things that hurt at this time was his bottom and his pride. Who knows how he got his bloody nose. There was a number of people running about, any one of these people could have knocked into PC Grey. One thing is for sure, the defendant didn't elbow PC Grey. How could he? When they stood face to face? How can you be sure they were face to face? In the words of PC Grey. He was trying to handcuff the defendant. When a suspect is arrested and put into a police car the cuffs are applied with the arms in front of the body. Some new health and safety policy, apparently. There must be at the very least reasonable doubt. As for the prosecutions claim, that the defence had influence the defendants pleas. Nonsense, Mr Watson, held his hands up to the other two charges, on his own accord.

Thank you ladies and gentlemen, I'm sure you will come to the correct, and only verdict possible in this case. Not guilty."

After judge Prior finished his summing up, and giving guidance to the jury, court was adjourned. The jurors were taken to a room to consider their verdict.

Jack sat in the canteen, with his brief.
"Which way do you think it will go Mr Baker?" A concerned looking Jack asked.
"It's too close to call Jack. What might tip the balance in your favour, is the testimony of John Ramsey. His little comical analogy, could prove to be priceless."

After two hours, the jury had a verdict. Back in the court, the foreman of the jury, was asked to stand, by the clerk of the court.
"Have you reached a verdict on which you all agree?"
 The foreman of the jury replied.

"Yes, we have." A piece of paper, containing the verdict was handed to judge Prior.

"On the charge of assaulting a police officer. Do you find the defendant guilty, or not guilty?"

"Not guilty." Jack puffed his cheeks and mouthed the words "Thank you," towards the jury.

Judge Prior then, thanked and dismissed the jury. The clerk called out. "Will the defendant please stand?" Jack stood tall.

Judge Prior. "Have you anything to say before I pass sentence?"

"No, your honour." Jack was praying for a suspended sentence and a fine.

Judge Prior. "For the charge of causing actual bodily harm, you will go to prison for eighteen months. For the charge of resisting arrest, you will go to prison for three months, The sentences are to run concurrently. Take him down." Jack was led away shaking his head, wondering where his new place of residency would be.

CHAPTER 27

Now.

Things couldn't be any better for Jack and Laura. They both sat on the edge of the bath, staring at the pregnancy test, waiting for the result. Hoping for two red lines. Laura was almost certain she was carrying their second child; her body was reacting in the same way as with Robbie. Tears were in Jacks eyes as the two lines began to appear on the small test panel. Laura gave out a loud yell of delight, as they hugged and danced around the bathroom.

Jack knew that Laura wanted a girl this time. Deep down so did he. They decided not to know the sex of the baby until the birth.

They had moved into their new four-bedroom house in Broxbourne, just two months ago. Still close enough to the river Lee, so they could enjoy the walks they both loved so much. They liked nothing better than to kick a ball around with little Robbie and hear him laughing loudly, as Jack chased after him in the open fields. Life was good for the little Watson family.

CHAPTER 28

Jack had been with STG, for just over a year. There was no mention of this anniversary. He expected a pay rise, as all his projects had exceeded expectations. This wasn't forth coming. Jack was of the view, that an employee shouldn't have to ask for a rise, in recognition for their performance. If the company appreciated, and indeed valued the employee, then this should be rewarded. Jack had received many "A well done," from senior management, not a word of congratulations from Brian Rice. But this didn't pay the bills. Jack like millions of other employees, felt undervalued and underpaid.

The project in Croydon, had started well and was still at the groundworks stage. Jack only visited twice a week, which he was grateful for because of the long drive. Another project, this one closer to home in Barnet, had just started. Jack was happy about this as it meant he spent less time in the office. Things were only marginally better now. The room still went quiet, whenever Jack walked in. Barry was still winding Jack up, always doing tomorrow, what should have been done today.

STG were getting lots of enquiries from potential clients, Jack was ultra-busy now. This suited him, as his day's seemed to fly by in the blink of an eye.

The site manager on the Barnet project, had booked a holiday the following week. Jack, once again saw this as an opportunity to get out of the office. On the pretence, that it saved the company money, Jack volunteered to baby sit the site. Steve readily agreed. Jack had arranged to pick up the keys from Barnet, on Friday afternoon.

On the Thursday, Jack got an email from Julian. The chance of a big contract had landed on his desk, and he wanted Jack to come to the office on Friday afternoon to discuss and do a program. It was unusual that Julian had chosen to email, instead of phone. Jack noted with interest that all senior management had been copied in. Attached to the email was the specification, and scope of works.

Jack responded to the email, copying everyone in. He told Julian he had arrange to pick the Barnet site keys up, tomorrow afternoon so he wouldn't come to the office. He had the information he needed to make a start on the program and they could catch up on Monday morning. This didn't go down well. Another email followed a few minutes later, informing Jack that Julian had instructed the site manager to bring the keys to the office. The email ended with the sentence, "Be in the office tomorrow at three." Jack was fuming. How dare Julian interfere with his plans. Jack had no intention of going to the office. He rang the site manager, Jeff, a relatively new employee and told him not to go to the office and stick to the arrangement already in place. He told Jack that Julian had phoned him just a few moments ago and insisted he brought the keys to the office.

"Please Jack, don't put me in a spot. I really need this job."

"Do what you fucking like." Jack hung up.

The next call Jack made was to Mike, his former employer. He asked Mike if the offer of the job was still on the table? Mike told him it was, and they agreed terms.

Jack broke the news to Laura, after Robbie had gone to sleep.

"I'm delighted Jack. What did Mike offer you?"

"The same as I'm on now, with the promise of a promotion once a difficult project was handed over."

"A promotion to what?"

"Projects manager, running multiple jobs. Plus, a five grand rise." Laura smiled and kissed Jack full on the lips.

"I love you my handsome man."

"I love you too Laura, very much."

Jack wrote and sent his letter of resignation that evening. He thought the months' notice he had to work was going to be interesting to say the least.

CHAPTER 29

Jack parked up outside the site in Barnet, at seven forty-five on Monday morning, the first day of his notice period. The main gates and offices had already been opened by Steve Ginn, who had messaged the arrangements to Jack early Saturday morning.

There were no warm greetings from either side. Steve asked. "So, tell me Jack what finally tipped you over the edge?"
"I thought that was obvious."
"Jullian?"
"Yes, that was the final straw. I am the contracts manager. I decide how the sites are run. I decide on the handover

of keys, not Jullian. That's the trouble with STG, everyone interferes in other people's jobs, instead of focusing on their own."

"I'm sure he didn't mean anything by it."

"You read the emails Steve. How dare he order me around? Anyway, my mind is made up, I'm off."

That's your decision Jack."

Steve went on to explain the notice period working arrangements. The first of four weeks was to be spent on site in Barnet. The remaining three weeks, were to be spent in the office, working alongside Jullian and Steve.

"So, no chance of gardening leave then?" Jack asked cheekily.

"What do you think Jack?" Steve replied with a wry smile.

"Just keep that prick Brian away from me. That's all I ask."

"He will be too busy celebrating to bother you." Steve said, now laughing loudly.

"How do you work with an arse like him?"

"He doesn't bother me Jack. I out-rank him."

Steve left site with a cheery, "See you next Monday."

Jack enjoyed his week baby- sitting the site in Barnet. He saw Brian's car parked up the road twice. But each time Jack approached he drove off. What a prick Jack thought. Even on his notice period that prick was checking up on him.

After handing back the keys to the returning, suntanned site manager, Jack walked into the office in Potters Bar at around eleven. It seemed even more frosty than usual. If that was possible. There was to be no comments of "Sorry to hear your leaving." Or "Good luck for the future Jack." That was for sure. Jullian was on two-week's annual leave, so Jack inherited his desk. He looked across at Steve. Who was trying to look busy. Jack thought there was no way he was playing the shoot the squirrel game with that pathetic little man. That's when Jack realised just how much he despised every one of his team. He was more convinced than ever that his decision to quit, was the correct one.

The next two weeks went by slowly. Each day seemingly dragging more than the last. Jack had completed the program, requested by Julian and handed it over to the surveyors for pricing. He was grateful for every opportunity to go to site. Even driving to Croydon was preferable, to sitting in the office. Steve informed Jack, that his final week of notice, would be given as gardening leave. The way Jack reacted to this news; you would have sworn he had just won the lottery. Steve asked Jack to leave the company phone, laptop and keys to the car. Jack refused, stating he had use of them until his contract was over.

"You can have all your property back on Friday." Steve was not impressed and walked off with a sigh.

Jack had three weeks until he returned to work for his previous employer. The first week, he spent pretty much recharging his batteries. Two rounds of golf, and several games of snooker, at his local club. On Friday morning Jack got an email from Steve Ginn. Instructing him to drop the car to the office before one o' clock, as he had arranged for collection. Jack replied immediately, stating that the car could be collected from his house after five o' clock, when his contract was over. I will leave the laptop and phone in the boot of the car and put the key on the front drivers side wheel. Jack knew this would piss him off, he was loving it. Two minutes later, another email from a clearly irate Steve.

"Jack, you are the most unprofessional man I have ever worked with. I hope you never ask for a reference from me." This made Jack smile and he replied, saying "why would I want a reference from a buffoon? Now go away you silly little man." That afternoon jack watched from his bedroom window as two cars parked opposite his house. He couldn't believe it. Jullian and Barry had been sent to collect the car.

Jack had surprised Laura, by booking a week by the sea in Bournemouth, just the three of them. Just before they set off, Jack checked his bank account. The payment he had received from STG. Was wrong. Way short of what he had been expecting. Instead of the three thousand four hundred Jack usually got paid. Only eight hundred and fifty had been deposited into his account. His payslip hadn't arrived. Jack decided not to mention this to Laura. He thought it must have been some kind of clerical error and he would sort it, after their trip to the South coast.

CHAPTER 30

Jack aged twenty-four.

After Jack's second experience of being incarcerated at her majesty's pleasure. He promised himself, that would be his last. He had served thirteen months, of the eighteen-month sentence, in Wormwood scrubs. A far cry from the cushy, by comparison borstal. He survived all the attempts of bullying, kept his head down and served his time. He used his free time wisely, studying construction site management.

Jack was working with a small builder based in Enfield, North London. He was doing well and was liked by management and co-workers alike. He was offered a promotion to site manager. After due consideration, Jack turned it down, instead opting for the lower position of carpenter foreman. This suited Jack as he still loved being on the tools. He enrolled in night school, to continue studying site management.

Jack played football with his local amateur team and had made several new and good friends. He also enjoyed playing golf and tennis. He had sub-consciously moved away from the pub culture he had grown used to. Jack gave up smoking weed. He felt, and indeed was a much better person. Another sport Jack found he had a natural talent for, was air rifle shooting. He bought himself a rifle, which shot either pellets or darts, depending on the competition. Before long he was winning tournaments in his novice class. He was best at short range, moving and pop-up targets. All of which were against the clock.

Once a month, the football club held a social night to raise funds. One of the best earners, was the virtual horse racing. There was always raffles, for various bottles of spirits and wine, also a few small cash prizes. At nine 'o clock, it was party time. The same DJ each night, big Dennis who played for the fifth team. Not the most gifted of footballers, Dennis stood six feet six tall and about the size of two average men. Behind the decks he was an expert, always engaging the crowd.

At one such event, Jack spotted a girl he hadn't seen before. He had difficulty taking his eyes off of her. She was sitting with a group he didn't know that well and he was too shy to go over.

Laura was sitting and laughing with her group of girlfriends. She noticed a fella looking at her more than once.

Each time she caught his eye, he quickly looked away. She thought that was sweet. She asked one of the girls, who the handsome chap was.

"Oh, That's Jack. Or Jack the lad, as we girls call him. Get in the queue Laura." Her friend Grace giggled. "We will see about that." Laura said laughing.

Greg, one of Jack's new best mates, noticed the attraction.

"She's a bit of a stunner Jack. You haven't taken your eyes off her for an hour." Greg said, teasing Jack.

"Do you know her mate?"

"Sure, That's luscious Laura. Come on I'll introduce you."

"Don't embarrass me Greg, or I'll punch you." Greg laughed at this, as they walked over to the group of girls. Greg announced.

"Laura, meet Jack. He thinks you are the best thing since sliced bread, but he was too much of a pussy to come over." Jack punched Greg in the arm and whispered in his ear, "You fucker." The girls all laughed, including Laura. Jack was glad of the dimmed lights, no one noticed him blushing. Mary, one of the girls stood up and said, "Why are you laughing Laura? You have been drooling over Jack for at least half an hour." This time it was the boys who chuckled. Laura gave Mary a look through clenched teeth. She too was reddening, but no one noticed.

Jack and Laura shook hands and began chatting. An hour or so later it was like they were alone in the room. Completely oblivious to all around them.

"Come on Jack, Let's dance." Laura said taking him by the hand, leaving him no choice but to follow her to the dance floor. They danced well together. Like it wasn't their first time. From opposite sides of the dance floor a group of boys and girls looked on in envy. Greg thought they made a lovely couple. Both bloody gorgeous.

Before the end of the evening just as cabs were being ordered. Jack asked.

"Can I see you again Laura? I have had a great time."

"Are you asking me for a date Jack?" Laura said with a cheeky glint in her eye. This was when Jack realised just how striking her green eyes were.

"Yes, I am Laura." Jack said quite seriously.

"That would be great." They exchanged phone numbers. Mary called Laura over as their cab had arrived. Jack held out his hand which Laura ignored. Instead, she gave him a kiss on the cheek and with a sexy wink she whispered.

"See you soon handsome."

Jack was blown away. He didn't sleep well that night, or indeed for several night's after. He didn't want to call her too quickly. In case she thought he was over keen. But on the other hand, he didn't want to wait too long in case she thought he wasn't keen enough. "What to do?" Jack asked himself over and over.

CHAPTER 31

Now.

On his return from Bournemouth, once Laura had left for work. Jack phoned STG; he spoke to HR about the shortfall in his final salary. After holding for a good few minutes, he was told that his payment was correct. Jack questioned this. HR said they would send over a breakdown of his hours for the last month, as logged by Brian Rice. Jack ended the call. Alarm bells were ringing.

He could not focus on his round of golf. So, he made an excuse at the seventh, saying he felt unwell. He rushed home and read the email from HR. Brian had done a right number on him. Claiming Jack was AWOL for most of his notice period. There was even a charge of three hundred pounds for the collection of the car. Plus, nine hundred for alleged damage to the car. Jack felt sick. He drafted an email back. Copying in Steve, Julian, Brian, Barry, and Adam the MD. Jack warned that if the missing two thousand five hundred and fifty pounds wasn't in his account in three days, he would take action that would cost STG a hell of a lot more.

Suffice to say, Jack heard nothing back from STG. He tried calling Jullian a couple of times, but he was unavailable. Jack had warned them, so he set about causing them some grief. He emailed all of the clients he had been involved with, stating his concerns over potential latent defects. Jack outlined poor installation methods and occasions where the engineers details were not followed. Adding that he pointed all these issues out at the time but had no confidence that they had been rectified. He knew that once STG got wind of this, the fireworks would begin. Meanwhile, Jack looked into taking STG to the employment tribunal to recover his lost salary. He filled out countless forms, and it soon became evident to Jack, that he didn't have any concrete proof to back up his claim. All he had was telephone and milage records. This concerned Jack. None the less he filed his claim to which STG responded and a date was set for the hearing. Jack had just a month to prepare.

A few days later, Jack received an email from Goldberg's. A solicitor, representing STG. They advised jack that he was in breach of contract, as he had signed a non-disclosure agreement. Any further breach would result in court proceedings against him. They also strongly advised Jack to get a solicitor. Jack, responded by thanking them for their advice. But as he didn't ask for it, they could stick it where the sun doesn't shine. As for court proceedings, Jack encourage them to go for it. He pointed out that "A duty of care." Trumped any non-disclosure agreement. He ended the email by instructing. "Do not contact me again."

Jack did a lot of research into past tribunal hearings, and the prospect of him winning was low. He wasn't going to give up, he intended to give STG as much aggravation as he could. Two weeks before the hearing date, Jack sent a final email entitled "Theft."

Good morning to the three stooges who stole from me. Steve Ginn, alias, poison dwarf. Brian Rice, alias, fireman Sam. And last but not least, the pretend director Julian Hajar.

I am offering you one last chance to do the right thing. Pay me my full salary and you will not hear from me again. If you don't, I promise you this, no matter what the decision of the tribunal is, I will cause all three of you grief.

Regards

The victim.

As Brian was reading Jack's email his mobile rang. It was Adam. Oh, great thought Brian.

"Good morning Adam, I take it you have read the email?"

"Yes Brian, I have. I am not happy. You caused this fucking mess Brian. Get it fucking sorted and be quick about it."

The line went dead. Brian was a bit miffed, He thought he was looking out for the company. He didn't consider the fact that he had developed an irrational dislike, bordering on hatred for Jack Watson.

CHAPTER 32

Jack aged twenty-five.

Jack and Laura had been dating for just over a year, He couldn't be happier. He had shared all his demons from the past. Laura was shocked to hear about his mum and dad. But by far the biggest loss to Jack, was that of his great mate, Peter. He still wasn't over it, even though more than eight years had passed.

Jack was having counselling from a woman recommended by Laura's mum. Rose was brilliant, not at all judgemental. She was in her early forties and still what Jack would call, a bit of a head turner. Tall blonde and very elegant. She had lost her own mother when only twelve. The counselling she got helped her so much that she chose that career path to help others. Jack could talk freely about his parents. He had learned to forgive his mum. She had an illness that had eaten her from the inside. He still loved her and was regretful that he didn't go to her funeral. Rose thought it would help for Jack to visit her grave, to tell her how he felt.

Jack went and spoke to his mum; he told her that he loved and missed her. And he hoped she had found piece wherever she was. On the other hand, Jack could not forgive his dad. He hated him with a vengeance. He was not ill. He was a lazy slob of a man. Nothing more than a bully. If the horse he backed had won, Jack was the best son in the world. But if it lost, which was more common, Jack would get a beating. The counselling had helped him to forget about his dad and leave the anger behind. Rose showed him how remembering Peter for the good times they shared, the father and son bond which they had. This also help Jack immensely every time he felt sad, or upset about Peter, He remembered the laughs they had and the joy of working together. Now, when he thought of Peter he would smile as opposed to cry. Rose also impressed on Jack the importance of talking about problems or issues that were upsetting him. "The worst thing was to bottle things up. You have to try to trust people Jack." She told him, "not everyone is a bad egg." Jack also admitted that he was reluctant to express his true feelings for Laura. All of his life the people he loved had, in one way or another hurt him. He wasn't going to let himself be hurt again. Rose asked Jack if he was in love with Laura. After several minutes, Jack admitted that he was. As he was leaving the session Rose said very calmly and very sincerely.

"To have any happiness, you will have to learn to trust again Jack. You love Laura, that much is clear. You're constantly talking about her. No matter what we are discussing, you always bring it back to Laura. Just tell her Jack."

He trusted Laura, that was for sure. He had shared all his feelings with her. She was a great listener and very caring. The emotional wall he had built, to protect him from being hurt, was crumbling brick by brick. He loved Laura like he had loved no other. He now had made the decision to tell her. He had to shake off this feeling of vulnerability. He told himself, "Let your heart go Jack."

CHAPTER 33

Laura absolutely adored Jack. She had lost her heart to him after two months. She couldn't tell him because he had built a wall, which she knew would eventually crumble. When the time was right, she would profess her love for Jack. In the early days of their romance, they saw each other once or maybe twice a week. Now they were together almost every day. Laura's parents thought the world of Jack, as did her sister Beth, who would often joke that if Laura ever got tired of Jack, she would happily step into her shoes.

Laura could see the change in Jack since he began his counselling sessions. She was shocked and saddened by the treatment he got from his parents. He had learnt that hating his dad was futile. Rose had told him that he was allowing his dad to hurt him still, although he was long dead. He spoke openly with Laura. She was so proud that he had agreed to counselling, it was changing Jack for the better.

CHAPTER 34

Jack spent the next couple of weeks formulating a plan of how to surprise Laura. He was not only going to tell her how much he loved her. He was going to propose. He didn't have a clue on what engagement ring to buy. He looked in countless jewellers windows. If the prices weren't on the display, Jack wouldn't have had a clue to which was the most expensive. He confided in Greg about his intentions. And his dilemma over choosing a ring.

"How the bloody hell am I to know which ring to choose mate? There are thousands."

"You're such a doughnut Jack. All you have to do is ask her mother."

"Greg you are a fucking legend. If Laura says yes. Will you be my best man?"

"It would be an honour mate. What do you mean if she says yes? That's a penalty kick. I would put money on it. She is mad about you. I can't see it myself. Your one lucky bastard Jack Watson."

Laura's mum, Gene, new exactly what she was looking for. Both daughters had pointed out their favourite rings on a girlie day out shopping. She pointed one out to Jack, in the first shop they went in. It was eighteen caret gold with three diamonds. The centre diamond was slightly bigger than the two set either side. Jack thought it was perfect and ordered it there and then. Gene had tears in her eyes when she said. "You're a lovely man Jack, you and Laura make the perfect couple." Jack thanked her and they hugged.

Part two of Jack's plan, which he Hadn't shared with anyone, was a city break to Paris. Laura had often mentioned how much she would love to climb the Eiffel tower. He booked a hotel close to the river Saine. This was expensive but he reasoned that Laura was the love of his life, so she was more than worth it. Jack would swear blind that he didn't have a romantic bone in his body. But on this evidence, he wasn't so sure. Laura was gobsmacked when she saw the Eurostar tickets on the table at breakfast. She threw her arms around Jack and kissed him ten times or more. She only just refrained from saying I love you.

"Three days in Paris with my handsome man, you are the best Jack."

Laura wanted to do some research so they could plan their days.

"There is no need darling, I have taken care of everything. All you have to do is pack a small bag and not worry about a thing."

Laura couldn't wait to tell her parents and

sister. They were all delighted for her. Beth teased her by singing a verse of "I'm getting married in the morning." their dad, Ray, chipped in with "Ding dong the bells are gonna chime." They all laughed heartedly, with Laura slightly blushing. Gene was the only one who really knew what lay ahead in Paris. It was difficult not to tell her husband, but she didn't want to risk any slip ups and spoil the surprise. Gene was so happy to see her eldest gleaming.

CHAPTER 35

As they boarded the train at St Pancras
station, Laura's jaw ached, she felt like
she hadn't stopped smiling for weeks.
The journey was only two and a half
hours in total, thirty-minutes spent in
the Chunnel under the channel. It was
just before mid-day when they got off
at Paris Gare Du Nord. Laura felt like
she was in a dream. Jack new exactly
where he was headed. They jumped on
the metro and headed for their hotel.
Laura was very impressed when she
saw the location. It was called, Hotel du
Danube Saint Germain and was only a
five-minute walk from the river Seine.

It was a beautiful day in Paris, a cloudless sky and bright sunshine. Jack took Laura by the hand. "Come on babe, first stop, the Arc De Triomphe." Laura could only smile and follow on. "You have it all planned, my handsome man." Jack had booked the entry tickets in advance. Laura was spellbound by the breath-taking view from above the Champs-e-Elysees at the top of the monument. "Look Jack, the city of love." She whispered.

The next stop was the Louvre. Both walked around in near silence as they observed the incredible array of artwork. The crowning moment was the Mona Lisa. Jack had commented earlier that he didn't know what all the fuss was about. But standing in front of it, he was beguiled by the way she seemed to be looking straight at him, only him and that tiny smile blew him away. Neither Jack nor Laura had considered themselves great fans of art, but they managed to spend over three hours spellbound by the magnificence of the place. Jacks second favourite piece was the Venus De Milo, while Laura's was the drawing of the wedding feast at Cana. She had stood admiring it silently for at least ten minutes. Jack, smiled to himself and thought their own wedding would be a little less grand.

The evening's entertainment was a meal in a quaint, traditional restaurant close to the river.

Laura ordered Bouillabaisse. "What's that? Asked a puzzled Jack. "It's a fish soup with lobster and clams and other types of fish thrown in." Jack wasn't a fan of fish so he went for the Escargot. When they were served, he didn't have a clue what he was supposed to do with them. The waiter noticed his awkwardness and demonstrated the method of removing the snail from the shell. "How are your Snails darling?" "They are a bit chewy but the garlic sauce is to die for." For the main course they both had coq-au van. Which was fantastic. There was no room for dessert. After a nice cognac, they strolled along by the river Seine, watching the moonlight dancing across the water. Jack thought, maybe he was romantic after all.

Day three was the big day. Although Laura was happily oblivious to what lay ahead. Jack was incredibly nervous. Standing in the long queue, waiting to access the Eiffel tower, Laura sensed something wasn't quite right. "Is everything ok darling? Your very quiet."

"Sorry babe, I'm just amazed by the size of the structure. It's an awesome feat of engineering." Laura wasn't convinced but she smiled and squeezed his hand. After lunch, in one of the two restaurants in the tower, Jack plucked up enough courage to go for it. Laura was finishing her coffee as Jack stood up and reached into his pocket. "I'll pay darling." She said, thinking he looking for his bank card.

Jack went down on one knee. Laura's eyes and mouth opened in shock.

"I love you Laura, with all my heart. Will you do me the great honour of becoming my wife?" Jack was aware that the restaurant had gone so quiet you could have heard a pin drop. Laura stood up with tears rolling freely down her cheeks. She held her palms outwards and said.

"Yes, I will Jack. I love you so much." As Jack put the ring on her finger, applause and cheers rang out all around the room. The waiter brought two glasses of champagne. Laura felt as though she was in a fairy tale.

The rest of the evening, Laura couldn't stop looking at her ring. Jack admitted that it was Gene who helped him pick it. She loved the fact that Jack had gone to so much trouble to make this the most precious moment of her life.

"I have loved you for so long my handsome man. I have been waiting for the right time to say those words." The Paris trip was over, but life was just beginning for loves young dream.

CHAPTER 36

Now.

On the morning of the tribunal hearing, Brian had called for a meeting, to ensure everybody involved was clear on the facts and evidence they may have to give. Only one representative from STG was required to attend. Brian thought that a show of strength would enhance their version of events. The rest of the group thought he was being way over the top. Present at the meeting were: Steve, Julian, Barry and John. Each had been tasked with gathering information about Jack's whereabouts during his notice period.

Brian stood as he addressed his somewhat bored audience.

"Gentleman, this is not personal. We must protect the companies interests and make sure we win this case. If we allow Watson to get away with this, where will it all end. We need to set a benchmark, send a statement to all employees of the company." Steve glanced at Julian who raised his eyebrows to the ceiling.

John asked, "Is it really necessary for Barry and me to be there? We have a lot on this morning in Barnet."

"For fuck sake John, how many times do we need to go through this? We are all going, end of conversation."

"Yes sir," John mumbled as he gave a mocking salute.

They were greeted by their solicitor, Mr Granger, when they arrived an hour early at the tribunal venue in Bloomsbury West London. Brian asked, "How do you think it will go Mr Granger?"

"It shouldn't have got this far, Mr Watson has absolutely no evidence to back up his claim. This will be thrown out in minutes. The judge would have read all the evidence before we go in." He expressed confusion as to why so many had come to the hearing. Julian and Steve again exchanged glances; this time both were looking up.

John had noticed that Brian had gone quiet, which was most unusual. He was watching the door. He said to Barry. "Look at the big man, he is shitting himself. I can't wait for Jack to walk in.

Jack was sitting in his office reading the sports section of his newspaper. He had no intention of attending a hearing he couldn't possibly win. He hoped it caused plenty of aggravation for the three stooges.

STG won the case, which was briefly heard in Jack's absence. Brian couldn't hide his delight; he acted like he had orchestrated a major legal victory. He looked like the cat who had got the cream. "I'd like to thank you all." he announced. "I knew we would nail that bastard. Come on, lunch is on me." On the way-out Brian called Adam, to break the good news. "Hi Adam, it was a formality, we won."

"That's good Brian. What did Jack have to say?"

"The little shit didn't turn up."

"Brian, I want Steve, Julian and yourself in my office at three o' clock this afternoon." The line went dead. Brian was unsure what to make of the call. Adam didn't sound annoyed but hardly elated either. Surely, he must be pleased at the outcome. Brian hoped this was the case.

At around twelve o' clock. Jack sent an email to Adam again titled "Theft."

Adam,

Let me be the first to congratulate STG, on their magnificent victory, secured this very morning, by the incredible three stooges. As you know this was a shallow victory. The cost to STG, far outnumbered the amount that you have stolen from me.

In real terms the victory is mine. Let the chaps know that I'm not finished yet. I want my money.

Regards

Jack Watson.

Brian didn't enjoy his lunch; He had a hint of indigestion as the three of them entered the board room. Already seated were Adam and Richard the surveying director. When they had taken their seats, Adam began.
"Brian, can you give a brief summary of the events, concerning Jack Watson?" This took Brian by surprise. He gave an outline of what had happened, concluding with the good news that STG had won the claim against them.

And he had saved the company around two and a half grand. Brian looked pleased with himself.

Adam turned to Richard and asked him to give a breakdown of all the costs accrued since Jack Watson had resigned from the company. Brian felt as though he was shrinking in his chair as Richard, reeled off the list.

"The cost of remedying the faults that Jack had made the clients aware of, Five thousand pounds. Legal fees to defend the claim, six thousand pounds. An estimate of time spent by Brian, Steve, Julian. Barry and John, collecting evidence and checking up on Jack during his notice period. Four thousand pounds."

"Thank you, Richard. Julian and Steve, you can both leave now. Rest assured I will be speaking to both of you on this matter very soon." They got up and left the boardroom without a word. Brian now looked physically ill.

"Brian you are a fucking disgrace. You have allowed your personal dislike for someone to cloud your judgement. Far from saving the company money because of your petty grievance, you have actually cost us well in excess of ten grand. Are you offering to pay that back?" Brian remained silent; he was clearly stunned.

"No, I didn't think so. I'm going to be straight with you Brian. I wanted to dismiss you for gross incompetence. However, because of our fathers close ties, I have been persuaded not to. If you had a grain of decency, you would resign today."

Brian coughed to clear his throat. "I'm sorry Adam, I admit I have made an error of judgement here. But I will not resign."

"A fucking error of judgement, are you fucking kidding me?" No response from Brian, who was now looking at the floor.

"If you ever let a personal vendetta, embarrass this company again, I promise you, I will sack you on the spot."

"It won't happen again Adam." Brian said under bated breath.

"You phoned me up to eulogise that we had won. Jack Watson is the only winner here. He's fucking laughing at you Brian. The same way he was laughing at you when he worked here. Sort yourself out Brian. Now get out. Brian went into the toilet and threw up. How he hated Jack Watson. He thought he had won, instigated his resignation, hit him where it hurts most, in the pocket. Yet still he felt like the loser, the idiot, the laughingstock of the company. And he was. The Brian Rice's of this world are controlling bullies, with, my way or the highway attitude. For the most part Brian got away with it. He just hadn't bargained on Jack Watson.

CHAPTER 37

The thought of the three stooges being smug and congratulating themselves, on what they may consider to be a moral victory, was really bugging Jack. He decided that he would get revenge on the protagonists. First on the list Barry. Jack didn't think he had much to do with the decision not to pay him, however he was convinced he certainly added fuel to the fire. Barry wasn't the real target of his anger but he needed to be taught a lesson anyway. Julian also wasn't his main nemesis, He sided with Jack in the early days, but soon showed his true colours when push came to shove. Yes, Julian also needed to be given some grief over his involvement.

The two remaining culprits, Steve and Brian were a different kettle of fish. It was personal with these two clowns, as Jack saw them. They would pay a much higher price than the amount they stole from Jack. You cannot put a value on the humiliation Jack was planning to inflict on the silly little man and fireman Sam. To get the ball rolling Jack paid an old mate of his, a hundred pounds to spray paint the word thief on the walls and front doors of the houses, owned by Steve and Brian. The addresses were easy to find as they were listed on the company records. Directors addresses are on there for all to see. He also wanted the same written on all cars parked on the drives. Julian's address however was not listed as he was only a pretend director. Jack would deal with him separately. His mate did as Jack had instructed and sent over the pictures to Jack's mobile. What a mess he had made, big red letters, he even added an exclamation mark which made Jack smile.

Jack knew that he might be suspected of this attack. There could be no proof so he wasn't unduly concerned. He deleted the images from his phone. Jack knew that Julian was an early bird and often would be at the office an hour before anyone else. One frosty morning Jack lay in wait. The car park was in darkness, completely empty. He was crouched behind a wall where he knew Julian would park. He didn't have to wait long. He pulled down his balaclava and armed with a baseball bat he was on top of Julian in a flash. The first blow to the back of the head had knocked him out. Jack went through his pockets and took his wallet and mobile phone. He ripped the watch off of Julian's wrist. Then just for good measure he smashed the baseball bat across the knuckles of his prone victim. He heard the bones crack. Then Jack, who was now in a cold rage set about Julian's car. When he left the damage was severe. "Thieving cunt." Jack whispered. Jack took the cash from the wallet then dumped it in the canal along with the phone and the watch.

Barry loved his motor bike, a vintage Harley Davison. Jack paid his mate two hundred pounds to smash the granny out of it. This time he instructed that no pictures were to be sent. Two scores settled and two to go. Jack hadn't quite decided on the extent of what lay ahead for the two clowns.

After the attack on Julian, the police were called in. The CCTV images were of no use. His injuries were not too serious. A couple of broken fingers and a headache for a week. Steve and Brian told the police about the paint attack on their houses. And also, the damage caused to Barry's bike. Brian also told them that he thought it was Jack Watson who was responsible. The police said they would look into it.

CHAPTER 38

Jack was smart enough to have an airtight alibi for when Julian was attacked. The site, he was running in Enfield had a fingerprint entry system. He accessed the site at six thirty, on the morning in question. This wasn't unusual for Jack. He knew there was a blind spot at the rear of the site. He climbed over the high wall and went about his business. Jack used the same way to get back into the site. When the other workers arrived, they could see Jack up on the scaffold taking progress photos as usual. The attack on Julian was at seven o' clock.

The police came to Jacks house, luckily Laura had taken Robbie to her mums. Jack of course, denied all knowledge and it seemed the police believed him. They said they would check the data from the finger scanner and that would clear Jack. When they left, Jack, hoped that none of the neighbours had been curtain twitching. He didn't want to tell Laura about this impromptu visit. Because of the police involvement, Jack thought it would be prudent to wait a few months, before inflicting revenge on Steve and Brian.

The next lesson That Jack had decided upon was to be a bit more painful for Brian and Steve. He felt that the punishments handed out to Barry and Jullian would suffice.

The time, and the place for his plan was simple. Jack parked his car a couple of streets away from the STG offices in Potters Bar. He got his air rifle out of the boot and a tin of darts; The gun was in a leather case which looked more like a snooker cue. He went to the fire escape at the rear of the offices. The door was never locked. Jack used this route in the summer. He often took his newspaper up and read it in peace and quiet on the roof. The management team at STG were creatures of habit. Every Friday morning, a two-hour project revue followed by bacon or sausage rolls from the mobile café in the car park. Jack looked at his watch, he only had five minutes to wait for his prey to appear. He loaded a dart and looked through the scope, he was only twelve meters up so he could read the menu clearly. Bang on time he herd the gang approaching. He could make out Brian and Steve, who walked side by side with his naked eye. Right, he thought, Brian first. The noise of the shot was drowned out by the generator powering the food wagon. Jack heard a yelp and then saw Brian hit the floor clutching his leg. Bullseye the dart landed in Brians calf. Initially no one went to his aid, they all stood looking at each other and shrugging shoulders. Steve was the first to react, he went down on his haunches to see what was wrong. This was too much of an opportunity for Jack to miss. Bang the second dart landed in Steve's ample arse. He jumped up with a squeal, Jack immediately thought about the squirrel game with Jullian, but this was for real. Steve hit his head on the serving hatch, which sent him crashing to the ground with one hand on his head and the other on his arse. Jack laughed as the others ran for cover, leaving their two workmates to their own devices. Jack couldn't stop laughing as he calmly packed his gun away and headed back to his car. There wasn't a sole about, all the excitement was at the front of the building.

CHAPTER 39

Work was going well for Jack; he was certainly a lot happier and more comfortable in the more familiar surroundings. Jack was not cut out to be a contracts manager. What he was cut out for was running his own business. He had bought some expensive woodworking tools and set himself up a workshop in his garage. Space was tight but he managed to make bespoke furniture, just like Peter had taught him. He worked a few hours in the evenings and all-day Saturday in his garage. He had picked up a few orders by word of mouth. Most popular were Welsh dressers and coffee tables. His clients loved them as they were one offs. He was making a nice few quid on the side. He told Laura of his plans to start up on his own. He had drawn up a business plan to present to the bank. He had found premises close to home, a good-sized warehouse unit in Enfield. He needed a bank loan to fit out the warehouse with all the tools necessary and also to buy a large transit van. Laura was very excited, and as usual very supportive in what Jack wanted to do. He told her there was no rush. First, he needed to build up a client base. The best way, he thought was to make some items and sell them at a craft fair. Laura who was a bit of a whiz on the computer said she would design business cards, and create a portfolio, show-casing Jacks furniture. She also set about designing a website. Jack was so happy that Laura was on board. He joked that once the business was established, he might offer her a job. If she had the right qualifications and necessary experience. Laura punched him on the arm and called him a cheeky sod.

Ahead of his first try at a craft fair, Jack had made several small items to sell. Ten plant holders with a circular top and three hand spun legs. Made from solid oak. Four, nests of three occasional small tables, made from mahogany and a couple of larger coffee tables made from teak. No screws were used in the making of the pieces. Proper joinery, as Peter said, on more than one occasion. Each item of furniture had been finished using bee's wax, which really showed off the natural grain of the wood. The hardest part for Jack was knowing what price tag to put on his items. Laura researched similar items offered for sale on the internet. This was a great help. The plant holders were priced at sixty pounds. The nest of tables, one hundred and fifty and the coffee tables at three hundred. Jack told Laura, that because it was a craft fair, there would almost certainly be some bartering involved. He didn't mind this, it actually added to the excitement. Jack would be happy to sell half of the items. This would more than cover the cost of the materials and make a tidy little profit.

Jack loaded a van, he borrowed from work, bright and early on the morning of the craft fair. Laura had offered to go along. Jack said he would be fine on his own. He gave her a big hug and thanked her for the wonderful portfolio she had produced.
"Knock them bandy, my handsome man." Laura said as Jack drove off.

Jack was a little apprehensive as he set up his pitch. A lady on the stall next to him noticed and offered him a cup of tea. Jack was delighted. The ladies name was Helen, she was a veteran of the craft fair world. She sold animals made from twisting bamboo. Jack thought they were brilliant. She soon made Jack feel at ease. He needn't have worried. Half an hour after the gates were opened, Jacks first customer bought four of the plant stands for the asking price, and congratulated Jack on his craftmanship. After three hours all that was left on Jacks stall was one of the large coffee tables. The rest had been snapped up. He loved it, people showed a genuine interest in how the furniture was made. His business cards were also going like hot cakes. He told Helen that he was packing up as he only had one item left. He joked that he would have to make a lot more for the next time. She was happy for him. Jack noticed that she too was having a good day, two thirds of her stock had been sold.

"You don't want to be taking that table back with you. I'll make you an offer."

"Go on," said Jack. "I'm all ears."

"I'll give you two hundred, plus you can pick one item from my stall." Jack smiled.

"Deal, I'll take the giraffe, my little lad will love it." They shook hands on the deal and Jack wished Helen good luck for the rest of the day.

Laura couldn't believe it when Jack called her with the news. She said she would put a couple of bottles of beer into the fridge and told him how proud she was. Jack had made over a thousand pounds profit. He needed to put a cost for his time against the return, but it was a much better start than he hoped. The next craft fair was in a months' time. The big thing for Jack was how much interest and potential orders would come in. Laura needed to get the web site up and running ahead of the next fair.

On the drive home, Jack thought about the happy times he had spent with Peter. How he wished he was here now to see his student excelling in the world of joinery.

CHAPTER 40

Jack aged twenty-seven.

In the two years since the trip to Paris, wedding plans had been at the top of the agenda. Laura wanted a big elaborate affair, she always dreamt of a fairy-tale type wedding. She was conscious of the fact that Jack had no family to invite. Indeed, he didn't have many friends either. When they spoke about it, Jack joked that the grooms side of the church would be a bit sparse. As for the brides side, people would have to fight for a seat. Laura said she didn't mind if they a had a small intimate affair, with just a few family and close friends. Jack wouldn't hear of it.

"I am marrying the most beautiful, most precious girl on this planet. Let's make it an occasion that will be talked about for years to come." Laura was so choked she couldn't speak. She fell into Jacks arms and stayed there for several minutes.

The week before the big day, Jack took off with Greg and three others from the football club. Destination Scotland. Greg had tried to convince Jack to have his stag do in Holland. Jack couldn't think of anything worse. Three days of playing golf at St Andrews, on the old course would be absolutely perfect.

Laura, her sister Beth and eight of her mates headed for Blackpool's golden mile, a very popular spot for hen parties. She looked the part on the train, wearing a brides veil and a sash bearing the bold letters of "Bride to be." The rest of the girls all wore matching pink tee-shirts with the words "Laura's hen crew on tour." Written on the back.

The first day of golf was a success for Jack. His handicap was twelve, by far the best of the group. The great thing about golf, is if you use the handicap system, all players have an equal chance to win. This of course is dependent on all players being honest. The other great thing Jack learnt early, was that very few people cheated. The golf course is a vast expanse and the occasional missed or scuffed shot would go unnoticed by your opponents. Each player kept their own score. If you cheated, you really only cheated yourself. Jack won by three shots, at twenty pounds a man, he had eighty pounds in his pocket as they headed to the clubhouse, known as the nineteenth hole. Jack paid for all the drinks before they headed back to the hotel for dinner. Soon after all were fed, the lads were keen to head off into town, Jack however told them he would prefer to stay in the hotel bar, he wanted to be fresh for an early tee off the following morning. The truth was that Jack wasn't a big drinker, two or three max. He saw at first hand the damage that alcohol can do to a person. He believed he lost his mother because of it. Jack encouraged the others to go and paint the town red, he would be fine. Greg stayed with him, he wanted to go, but he thought it would be better to stay. He was the best man after all.

At seven the next morning. Only Jack and Greg prepared to tee off. the others were far too hungover to contemplate eighteen holes. Two of them had black eyes.

Laura and her crew were having a great time. They spent most of the day at Blackpool pleasure beach. All screaming at the top of their voices while enjoying the rides. Before dinner all of them got on donkeys, a kind of tradition in Blackpool. Hundreds of pictures were taken, not all flattering. The crew spent the evening dancing the night away at Pop world nightclub.

Making the most of the two for one cocktails offer.

When Laura went to bed, she saw a text message from Jack.

"I love you, Laura. I can't wait until Saturday. Sweet dreams. Jack XXX."
She replied.

"I love you too, my handsome man. I can't wait to become Mrs Watson. XXX."

CHAPTER 41

Jack and Greg stood in the glorious early afternoon sunshine outside St Joseph's church, in Highgate. The wedding guests were beginning to arrive. Gene was also on hand to hand out the flowers and point the guests to their seats. They were told to sit either side just leave the front two rows on the right-hand side free. These were for the families.

Jack spent the night before, at Greg's house. They had an early meal, cooked by Greg's wife Ann. She spent the early part of the evening teasing Jack about how nervous he was. She had been close friends with Laura for a number of years. All three watched a film while drinking a few bottles of Budweiser.

Laura spent the evening at home with her parents. This would be her last night in the family house. She knew it would be strange, even though she had spent most of her nights with Jack over the past few months. She would take only happy childhood memories with her. Along with her mum, dad and sister Beth, she spent a lovely evening sipping champagne and reminiscing.

Five minutes before the bride was due to arrive, all the guests were seated. Jack's hands were sweaty and his legs felt a little weak. He looked up at the altar, where two seats had been set facing the congregation. Laura thought it would be nice for people to see their faces and not just the backs of their heads. Jack thought it was a good idea at the time, now he wasn't so sure.

He was shaken from his thoughts, by the organ announcing here comes the bride. Everyone turned to face the entrance. Laura walked in, looking every inch a princess. She linked her proud dads arm as they made the slow walk up the aisle. The white dress really enhanced her figure. Beth was behind holding the train of the dress. Jack squeezed Greg's arm; a lot harder than he intended. Gene was in floods of tears in the front row along with several other members of the family. It was all Jack could do to hold back his own tears.

Laura joined Jack at the front of the church and they walked together and stood by their seats waiting for the priest to begin. Jack whispered. "Laura you are the most beautiful woman in the world. I love you so, so much."
Laura smiled and kissed him on the cheek. This brought a little chuckle from the crowd. The happy couple exchanged their vows without a single

hiccup. Then after the photographs it was off to the reception. A sit down three course meal for all one hundred and forty guests wasn't cheap at sixteen pound a head, but the quality of the food and the efficient service made it more than worth it.

The speech's followed, beginning with Laura's dad. Ray was very relaxed and handled the microphone like a professional. He started with the old gag of can all Laura's ex's please return the keys to the house, to which at least ten lads got up and handed keys in at the top table. Then he went on to talk about his little princess, and how it seemed like only five minutes ago that he was changing her nappies. Laura blushed a little but no one noticed. Jack was taken by surprised when Ray spoke about him. He was choked by the lovely sincere welcoming words used. After Greg's ten-minute routine which was mainly based on how it was down to him, that the happy couple were here today. He quipped that if it were left to Jack none of this would have happened.

The dance floor was clear, when the DJ called for the bride and groom, to have the first dance. It took them a while to make their song choice. It seemed all the classics were about the man declaring his love for the woman. Greats like Perfect by Ed Sheeran, Three times a lady by Lionel Ritchie and Always and for ever by Heatwave. Jack and Laura wanted a song that declared love, from both partners. They chose I got you babe by Sonny and Cher. The guests cheered and clapped as they sang the words to each other, not breaking eye contact throughout the whole dance.

The evening was full of people offering their best wishes. Jack found it hard being in the limelight, while Laura seemed to be thriving on all the attention.

Jack managed to get a few minutes on his own, Laura was up dancing to the locomotion. He grabbed himself a cold pint of lager and sat down. He couldn't stop himself from smiling, as he watched the love of his life strutting her stuff.

"Shove up Jack, make room for a little one." It was Beth, she was clearly full of high spirits, her eyes were slightly glazed.

"Sit down sister, how are you enjoying the day?"

"It's great Jack. Are you enjoying it though? It looks like hard work to me." Jack laughed.

"Yeah, it's a bit full on. But I'm the luckiest man in the world."

"Laura is the luckiest girl in the world if you ask me. I wish I could find a fella like you Jack." This took him by surprise, it must have been the drink talking.

"Your gorgeous Beth. You must have fellas chasing you the whole time?"

"You're so sweet Jack, you don't have to say that. I'm a grown up."

"I mean it Beth. I have just married your sister, who to my mind, is the most beautiful woman I have ever seen. The two of you could easily pass as twins, so I know what I'm talking about." Jack thought they looked the same, however the personalities were Wildly different. Laura was mature beyond her years, whereas Beth was still very childlike in her ways even though there was just two years between them.

"So that must make me the second most beautiful woman you have ever seen?" She said with a saucy wink. Jack laughed. "I guess so."

Beth, looking serious now, leant in close to Jack. "I wish I had found you first." Jack didn't know what to say. Laura came over just in time. "And what are you two gossiping about?"

Beth got up and gestured for Laura to sit down. "I was just telling Jack how lucky you are." Then she walked off giving Jack a cheeky smile. "What was all that about Jack?"

"Darling, I have no idea, she has clearly had a few too many."

Beth walked over and sat with her mum and dad. Ray had taken his tie off and his unbuttoned shirt showed off his hairy chest. He was sweating from far too much dad dancing. He looked at their beautiful daughter and her new husband. Love was a powerful thing. Ray put his arm around Beth, feeling she may be a bit jealous. "Your time will come my princess."

The cab that Jack ordered, arrived bang on time to pick them up and take them to the Hilton hotel at Gatwick airport. Their flight to Acapulco Bay wasn't until the morning. As Jack and Laura got into the cab, the cheers and whistling were deafening. Fourteen nights in sunny Mexico lay ahead. They couldn't be happier.

Beth, on the other hand wasn't so happy. She couldn't sleep. Why was she so jealous of her sister? Laura always did better at school and was better at sports, in fact she outshone Beth in everything. everyone loved Laura. Beth didn't realise, that this was the case because Laura was far more outgoing than her. Laura was very tactile and would always greet her friends and family with a hug. Whereas Beth was more aloof and would be happy with handshakes and air kisses. Now to make matters worse Laura had Jack and she had no one. Beth wanted to be happy for her sister, she hated feeling so jealous. Laura had only ever shown her love. Beth had a crush on Jack, she knew she had to shake it off before it went too far.

CHAPTER 42

Now.

Jack's second visit to the craft fair was to be even more fruitful than the first. This time he took twice as many items of furniture and sold all but two pieces. Even more promising was the amount of quotes for private customers he had been asked to do. Most were for side boards and Welsh dressers. Two asked for a price to supply and fit solid oak kitchens.

Jack and Laura had drawn up a business plan, that Jack was to present to the bank. He booked the day of the appointment off from work. His meeting with Mr Davison was at ten o'clock. The same time he had arranged for his old pal to pay another visit to the houses, of both Steve and Brian. Same M.O. Cause mayhem with a can of spray paint. Just a little reminder to them that their theft was far from forgotten. Jack would have the perfect alibi if the police came calling. Jack thought it was worth paying another two hundred quid to teach those shyster's a lesson. He told his mate not to send any photos. But arranged to meet up in the pub later that afternoon. If Jack was happy with the carnage, he would hand over the money.

Mr Davison the branch manager saw Jack on the stroke of ten. Jack asked for a twelve thousand pound loan. He explained what the money was for. He listed the tools he needed to get the business up and running. A router, a chop saw, a bench saw, a circular saw, a coping saw and an electric planer. Mr Davison, nodded along to the list like he understood what Jack was talking about. He was very impressed with the amount of orders Jack already had on his books. He decided to lease a van separately. Jack had forecast rising profits year on year for the next three years. Initially he would only employ an apprentice but hoped to get more staff as the business expanded. Mr Davison agreed the loan and was satisfied that Jack could make the monthly repayments over two years. He also offered Jack a top up loan after six months if he needed to buy more equipment. The value of the two kitchens, Jack had been asked to make was over twenty-eight thousand. Each would take Jack four weeks to make. Both clients were happy to pay twenty five percent up front to cover the cost of materials.

With the loan in place, he set off on his second mission of the day. He put a deposit down on an industrial unit in Enfield. And agreed to take ownership in six weeks. This gave him time to order all the machinery he needed and work his months' notice. Jack wasn't looking forward to breaking the news to his boss. They had been good to him. But Jack knew it was time to go on his own. He also booked in a sign writer. J Watson & Family. Bespoke joinery Ltd, had a nice ring to it. He phoned Laura, who was just as delighted as Jack. She had lots of ideas for advertising the business, in the weeks leading up to Jack starting in the warehouse. She had already ordered one thousand fliers to be dropped through letterboxes, she also planned to put adds in the local papers the week before the grand opening.

Mid-afternoon, Jack met up with his spray paint mate Paul. He showed Jack the pictures from the scene. Jack laughed when he saw the damage, it was worse than the first time. Paul mocked, that both houses had installed doorbells with cameras. He painted those first, followed by the security cameras. Jack paid him the money. Paul asked, if jack wanted them hurt. He would gladly break a bone or two if the price was right. Jack declined this offer and told Paul he would deal with those thieves in his own time and in his own way.

The respective wives of Steve and Brian had called their husbands along with the police. Again, they put forward the name of Jack Watson, as the prime suspect. "It has to be him. He has made threats in emails. He has to be stopped." Brian was almost shouting at the police. The police said they would look into it.

Jack and Laura had a nice evening meal, washed down by a couple of chilled glasses of Champagne. Neither of them were overly keen on champagne, but they felt it was right for their celebration. "To The Watson family." Jack and Laura toasted.

A few days later the police called Brian to inform him, he was wrong about Jack Watson. Who was with his bank manager at the time the offence was committed. Brian was not happy. He went into Steve's office and told him the news. "When will he stop?" Steve asked shaking his head.

"Perhaps we should send Watson a message of our own, do we know where he lives Steve?"

HR should have an address, what do you have in mind?"

"I'm not sure. We can't allow him to keep getting away with it. It's costing a small fortune to get that paint cleaned off."

"You don't have to tell me about it, my misses is going mad. She keeps asking why we are being victimised."

"What have you told her?"

"The truth. That is was being done by a disgruntled employee, who had felt cheated out of his salary. She even suggested we just pay him the money and put an end to it."

"It's gone too far for that now Steve. It would be like admitting to wrong-doings. Leave it with me, I'll come up with something."

"I'm not sure Brian. It could make a bad situation worse."

"Nothing too dramatic Steve just a

message to warn him off. We have to

put a stop to this."

CHAPTER 43

Jack's boss was a little disappointed with the news that Jack was setting up on his own. He fully understood and wished him well in this new venture. Saying he was more than confident; Jack would be very successful.

Things were quiet on site; Jack used the time to order all the plant he needed for the grand opening. He also procured all of the oak required for the two kitchens. Jack offered his clients a big saving if he used a chipboard to make the carcases of the wall and base units. Neither wanted this, insisting on oak being used everywhere. Money it seemed, was no object to certain people.

Jack found an ideal apprentice, the son of one of the on-site carpenters. Jeff was seventeen and full of enthusiasm. Jack offered him a trial period. Working on Saturday's and Sunday's in Jack's home workshop. Jeff was so good, and obviously skilled for his age, Jack paid him for his efforts and offered him the job on the first weekend.

Jack still had two weeks, between his notice period and taking possession of the warehouse. He used this time, along with Jeff, to make items for the next craft fair. Jack, needed to keep this side of the business going, not only for the publicity and passing trade. The revenue from the sales would comfortably cover the repayments on both the bank loan and the lease for the van. He had explained to Laura that for the first few months, he would need to work long hours. Once the two kitchens were fitted, he could then look to take on a couple of joiners, this of course was dependent on securing new orders. It was going to be very challenging for Jack. Along with the workload, he also had to prepare the quotes. Thank goodness Laura was taking care of the accounts. She was very meticulous, every penny needed to be accounted for. The landlord of the warehouse was very accommodating because the unit was vacant, he allowed Jack to start the fit out before his tenancy date. This was a great help. Jack would be able to crack on with the orders in the first week of business. All the plant and materials were delivered on time. Jack was now itching to get started. Laura had convinced him to take the weekend before the opening off. As God only knew, how long it would be before the next opportunity. Jack booked a round of golf on the Saturday and arranged a boys day out with the gang that went on his stag do. The plan for Sunday was a trip to the seaside with Laura and Robbie.

Laura was six months pregnant, but you would never have guessed. Like with Robbie, she wasn't very big until the last two months. Barely a bump.

CHAPTER 44

Jack, Greg and the boys had a smashing day for a round of golf. The sun was shining and there was very little wind. The greens were lightening quick. This didn't suit Jack's putting stroke. His method was to attack every hole. If the ball dropped, all well and good. If he missed it, Jack's ball would go ten feet past and he would end up with a bogey, or worse. Jack really enjoyed the morning, even though he came last. He felt totally relaxed. The boys headed to the club house for some refreshment.

The bar was busy, it was the annual awards presentations. Jack was up for a trophy for his win in a Stapleford competition earlier in the year. Greg went to the bar while the others grabbed one of only two free tables. The talk soon turned to Jack's new adventure. Greg told Jack he would be a great success, "If I only had half of your ability mate, I would be more than happy."

Loud laughter and cheering drew Jack's eye to a table near the door. This crowd had been very successful, there were five trophies on the table. Jack had to look twice, it couldn't be, could it? It fucking was. Steve Ginn, laughing with the crowd. His laughter stopped the moment he saw Jack looking at him. Jack stared a hard cold stare for a couple of minutes. Making sure he didn't blink. He knew it was making Steve uncomfortable by the way he was shifting around in his seat. Jack's initial thought was to make a cunt out of one the three stooges. Who in their wisdom thought it was a good idea to steal from him. This wouldn't go down well with the club's committee, and because Jack enjoyed his golf so much, he didn't want to jeopardise his membership.

Jack looked away, and bided his time, until Steve either went to the bar, or the toilet. Then he would go and say hello. Around ten minutes later, Jack glanced back to the table. He was surprised to see Steve was no longer seated but was headed towards him. "Hello Jack, fancy seeing you here." Steve said with a little chuckle. Jack remained cold faced. "Maybe we better talk outside Steve, I don't want to cause a scene in here." Jack nodded towards the exit. Steve's face changed to one of concern.

Once outside and away from prying eyes and ears, Jack cut to the chase. "Why did you cut my salary Steve?" "It wasn't my idea; Brian had this bee in his bonnet that you were taking the piss during your notice period. He resorted to spying on you and getting others to do the same."

"You were my line manager, you're the one who signed my time sheets?"

"I know Jack, I had no choice, Brian backed me into a corner and pressured me into going along with it."

"So, your telling me, you were bullied?"

"Yes Jack, along with Jullian and Barry. Brian can be very persuasive."

"I gave you all the chance to do the right thing?"

"I know Jack, but it had gone too far. If it makes you feel any better, Brian got a proper rollocking from Adam, he was asked to resign over the amount of money his obsession with you had cost the company."

"That's something I suppose. It doesn't get me my money back though, does it?"

"I'll make a deal with you Jack, if you stop spray painting my house, and taking pot shots at me, I will pay you the money myself."

"I don't know what you're talking about Steve," Jack said with a grin and raised eyebrows.

"That's a very generous offer. You are only responsible for half of the money. I will accept twelve hundred and fifty from you. Then you will hear no more about it from me?"

"OK Jack you have a deal, let me take your account details."

"No mate, it has to be cash. I don't want you telling the wrong people that I'm blackmailing you."

"Fine Jack I just want to put a stop to this; my wife is going ballistic."

"Show me your phone Steve."

"What, why?"

"Just give it to me." Steve handed it to Jack, who looked at it and tossed it back.

"You can't be too careful Steve. I wouldn't want our little chat recorded now would I?"

Steve had a look of exasperation. "You don't have much trust, do you Jack?"

"Are you surprised? The way STG treated me. Bring the cash next Sunday lunchtime. And be very discrete Steve." "I will. Just a word of warning, Brian is planning on some kind of revenge on you. He has been trying to find out where you live." Jack laughed at this. "Tell him he better not come alone." With that, both Steve and Jack returned to their respective tables and carried on as if nothing had happened. There was no more eye contact between the two.

Greg asked Jack where he had disappeared to. He made out he had to give Laura a call, about the new business.

Jack thought about the warning Steve had passed on. The good news was, he didn't update his details with STG when he moved. That dickhead Rice would be heading to the wrong house.

CHAPTER 45

At ten thirty on the day before the grand opening of the Watson and family business. Jack, Laura and little Robbie arrived in Brighton. They loved this place, the only thing that annoyed Jack was the cost of parking for the day. It was probably cheaper to travel by train when you added the cost of the fuel to the parking. For the first two hours, Robbie happily splashed about in the water. Screaming while being chased by his dad. The Brighton Sea is notoriously cold, somehow children seemed oblivious to this. By the time they decided to get some lunch, Jack's feet were numb.

Wetherspoons was cheap and cheerful, not the best quality of food, but certainly great value for money. Neither Laura nor Jack had alcohol. Laura was of course pregnant and Jack was driving. He had had enough the previous day at the golf club and wanted a clear head for the start of their new adventure the next day. After lunch they strolled along the pier, a walk they had done numerous times in the past. Most visitors, it seemed, walked up and down the pier at least twice a day. Robbie loved the little rides; his favourite was sitting in a cup and saucer. For some reason he couldn't get enough, the imagination of children knows no boundaries. They spent the final few hours by the sea, walking up and down the promenade. Laura suggested a ride in British airways viewing tower, they decided against it as the sky was too cloudy. Robbie fell asleep on the journey back to London and Laura put him straight to bed when they arrived home.

Jack and Laura couldn't focus on the film they had put on. The new start was all they could think of and talk about. Jack emphasised that for the first three months, he would need to work seven days a week, then things should be up and running smoothly. Laura squeezed his hand and whispered that she had every confidence in her handsome man.

CHAPTER 46

Jack picked up young Jeff early Monday morning. It was clear to see the kid was bursting with excitement. Jack remembered how he was with Peter. They got to the industrial unit at seven thirty, Jack had told Jeff that from tomorrow onwards he would have to make his own way as Jack intended to start work earlier each day. Jeff said he didn't mind starting early too. "No mate your time is eight to five. I'll cover your fares." When the lights were switched on Jack stood and looked at his spotless, spacious well stocked unit. He rubbed his hands together and said. "Right Jeff my lad, let's get cracking, here is the plan. In the run up to opening Jack had made enough items for the next two craft fairs, which were stored in his garage. He had also drawn up a cutting schedule for the first of the two kitchens. He explained to Jeff that for the first morning he was to watch him cutting the oak to the sizes required to make the kitchen cupboards. Jeff had worked on bench saws at college, where he spent one day a week, he was two years into his apprenticeship. He was confident that he could use the machine straight away. But agreed with Jack, saying he thought it was a good idea. By lunchtime, Jack had cut enough oak to form all of the base units. Jeff had lost count of the number of times Jack repeated the importance of not marking the wood." This is the finished product Jeff, all it gets is wax, the least little mark or dent and it will be rejected. These clients are paying a lot of money and they require perfection." Masking tape was used to number and label the pieces. The plan for after lunch was for

Jack to cut all the mitres ready for assembling. Jeff was to cut the oak for the wall units. He had watched how organised Jack was, cut one, label it, number it and tick it off the cutting list. Jack smiled to himself as he watched jeff scoff his lunch in ten minutes, the young fellow couldn't wait to get cutting. "Take your time mate, your gonna choke. You need to relax for half an hour, the saw, and the wood won't mind waiting for you." Jack thought that young Jeff was going to be an asset.

CHAPTER 47

Steve Ginn was true to his word and gave Jack twelve hundred and fifty pounds in the car park at the golf club. "So, jack, is that an end to it? Are we all square?" Steve offered Jack his hand. "Yes, there is no more to be said on the matter, you should have done it months ago. It would have saved a lot of grief." Jack shook his hand. "Just one more thing Steve, what pub does Brian drink in?" "He goes to the gate in Hertfordshire, every Saturday lunchtime, but you didn't hear that from me."

Work on the first of the oak kitchens was ahead of schedule. Jack had estimated four weeks, but with his young helper all the units were made in three. He had a free week, before he could fit the kitchen as agreed with the client. The first couple of days were used to cut all the materials for the second kitchen. Jack called the client, who was delighted to hear that Jack could fit his kitchen a week earlier than the date that had been pencilled in.

The rest of the week Jack could use to catch up on all the enquiries and quotes he had in his diary. He left Jeff at the warehouse to prepare the items for the upcoming craft fair. He gave him the strict instruction not to use any of the cutting machines while he wasn't around. Jeff had no need to, as all the cutting and joint preparation had been done.

Laura was now eight months pregnant and was working from home. She was startled by a loud knocking on the front door. From the shapes outside the glass panel, she knew it was the police. Her first thought was something has happened to Jack. She was shaking as she opened the door.

"Mrs Watson?" Asked a burley policeman with a black bushy beard. He was accompanied by a slender girl, so young she must have been a new recruit.

"Yes, I am. What's happened? Is it Jack?"

"It's Jack we have come to see, I take it he is not home?"

"No, he is at work. Can I help?"

"There has been an incident at your former address, the front of the house has had paint smeared all over the walls, doors and windows. Just one word was written, Stop."

"What has that got to do with us?"

"We believe jack, could well have been the target." The policewoman added.

"What, how? I don't understand."

"Do the names Steve Ginn and Brian Rice mean anything to you?

"I've never heard of them, who are they?"

"Former colleagues of your husband, both have been victims of two similar graffiti attacks on their houses. We questioned your husband about it at the time, as the victims had suggested him as a suspect because of some pay dispute."

"I have no idea what you are talking about." Said Laura becoming increasingly angry.

"Ask you husband to drop in at the station later today, we would like to ask him a few questions." Laura said she would. Closing the door, she thought "I would like to ask him a few bloody questions as well." She decided to give herself ten minutes to calm down, before she called Jack.

Jack had just left a big house in Hampstead, where he had secured a valuable order for two Welsh dressers and a coffee table the size of a dining table but with shorter legs. He was surprised to see Laura's name on his phones display. She rarely called him at work.

"Hi babe, what's up?"

"The police have just been here Jack; they want to talk to you today at the station."

"What is it about, did they tell you?"

"Yes, our old house has been vandalised by someone with a tin of paint. They think you may know something about it. Do you Jack?"

"Why should I know anything?"

Jack don't lie to me. They told me about your former colleagues who have also been the victims of similar attacks. They gave your name to the police as a potential suspect." Jack remained quiet, silently gritting his teeth.

"Why didn't you tell me about this?"

"I didn't want to worry you love; it was nothing. They asked me a few questions before but I had an alibi for both attacks."

"They also talked about some kind of dispute about your pay, you didn't mention that either?"

"My pay was a little less than I expected and I sent a couple of sarcastic emails, that's all."

"We said there were to be no secrets Jack, didn't your counselling teach you that?"

"That's not fair Laura, this was so petty I thought it wasn't worth mentioning. I'll tell you all about it later, after I go and talk to the police."

"Ok Jack, I'll see you later. But please Jack, no secrets, however small they may seem to you."

"Ok babe, bye." Jack was furious, fucking Brian Rice. He thought I need to sort that prick out.

Jack was in and out of the police station in fifteen minutes. He told them he knew nothing about it, maybe they should be talking to his accusers. It was obvious to Jack that this had to be the doings of Ginn and Rice. The police told him, that like Jack, they too had airtight alibis.

Jack smoothed things over with Laura. He apologised for not telling her about the incident with the police and said it wouldn't happen again. Even though he knew this was far from finished. He hated Brian Rice with a passion that was growing.

CHAPTER 48

The next morning things were going to get worse for Jack. He had only been on the road for an hour, after setting up Jeff at the warehouse. He had two house calls to make, both were interested in his plant holders and tables. The website, that Laura had designed and set up was bringing in regular enquiries. And the order book was filling up, Jack had enough work to see him through the next six months, he really needed to employ at least one more joiner.

Jack's mobile rang, it was Jeff. I hope he hasn't had an accident was Jack's first thought.

"Jeff, how's it going?" Jeff's voice was shaky, he was stuttering, almost crying. "Calm down mate, I can't understand you."

"Two blokes came in armed with baseball bats, they said to give you a message".

"Are you ok Jeff? Did they hurt you?"

"No, I'm fine, they scared the shit out of me though."

"What was the message?" Jack already had an inkling.

"They said the message was from the fireman, This bollox stops here before it goes too far. What does it mean boss?"

Don't worry about it Jeff, it's just some idiot, I will sort it out. Did they cause any damage to the machines or the stock?"

"They wrote STOP on one of the coffee tables".

"Ok mate, listen, not a word to anyone about this. I don't want my wife or your parents worrying. Trust me it won't happen again. I won't be leaving you on your own again mate." This made Jeff feel happier.

"If you feel a bit shaky, lock up and go home."

"Thanks boss, I'm ok now."

Jack hung up. He sat in his car with his head in his hands, he was raging. First the old bill come knocking and upsetting Laura, now this. A visit to the Gate public house was called for. One or two things needed to be said to that cunt Rice.

CHAPTER 49

Jack parked outside the Gate public house, ten minutes before opening time. He sat and watched the punters arriving, mostly middle-aged men with newspapers tucked under their arms. After around half an hour, a few couples were going in, it was a nice country pub, very big and served food. The next car that pulled in, and parked four spaces from where Jack was watching, belonged to the man responsible for his being there. Brian Rice, accompanied by who Jack assumed to be his wife, and another couple of a similar age. The four were so well dressed, they could have been heading to Royal Ascot. Jack watched them go in, trying to stay calm. Remember where you are Jack, he told himself, just say what you came to say and leave. He knew that he couldn't afford to lose his temper, that prick would call the police without a second thought. He waited another twenty minutes then casually strolled through the door. He went to the bar and ordered a half of lager. As he looked around, he spotted the happy foursome, merrily chatting away and looking at the menus.

As Jack approached the table, Brian spotted him. The happy face was gone in an instant, he looked a worried man. "Good afternoon, Brian how the devil are you? my old mate." His words were louder than they needed to be. The table and indeed the tables in close proximity went quiet.
"What are you doing here Watson? What do you want?"

"The name is Jack; you always were an arrogant knob." His voice was still raised and more tables became quiet.

"I said what do you want Watson?" Brian was showing a bit of bravado, which took Jack by surprise.

"I'm here to give you some friendly advice, we can go outside and discuss it if you would prefer, I would rather not embarrass you in front of your family and friends."

"Whatever you have to say Watson, you can say it here. Be brief will you, our lunch will be along shortly." His smugness was really getting to Jack, but he remained calm, and with a smile he began.

"Firstly, you are responsible for me not getting my correct salary. You even resorted to spying on me, you sad fuck." Brian interrupted.

"Keep the language down, there are ladies present. You took the piss; I caught you out, so deal with it."

"Steve Ginn offered to pay me the full amount that was stolen from me."

"Your lying."

"I only accepted half of the money from him, because you owe the other half."

"I don't believe you Watson."

"How do you think I knew where to find you?"

The penny seemed to be dropping.

"Yes, Steve told me, and he also told me that you got a roasting from The MD at STG for causing me to leave. You were asked to resign." Brian was now looking embarrassed.

"He is talking nonsense; he is a bitter former employee who got found out."

"What about the two henchmen you sent to terrorise my apprentice? That was very brave."

Brian now knew he had to go on the attack, everyone was staring, and Jack was enjoying every minute. He was looking foolish.

"Let's talk about how brave you are Watson. Sending someone to spray paint our houses in the dead of night and shooting at us from some hideout, yeah very heroic."

271

"You would know all about that Brian, shame you got the wrong house. If you call me Watson one more time, I will take you outside and show you which one of us is brave." The bar manager came over and asked Jack to leave, or he would have to call the police.

"There is no need, I'm going. If you send anyone else to see me, I swear I will fucking shoot them, Then I will come for you. You stole from me and I won't forgive or forget that. You are a cunt of a man." With that Jack headed for the exit. No one inside the pub spoke until he left.

"Fuck you Watson, and the horse you rode in on." Brian tried to laugh it off, referring to Jack as a bit of a loose cannon. But it was clear from his face that he was not blameless, everyone could see that. Brian knew when he got home, he would have to undergo a thorough interrogation from his wife. Not something he was looking forward to, she could be like a dog with a bone. Mrs Rice was not easily fobbed off.

Another confrontation lay in wait for Monday morning, this one less daunting. He couldn't believe that his own colleague had sold him down the river. The trouble with Brian Rice was that he was oblivious to just how unpopular he was in most circles.

Jack drove off in a hurry in case the police had been called. He felt he had let himself down, by losing his temper at the end. It wasn't smart, throwing threats around in public, too late to change that now. He also knew that he had thrown Steve Ginn under the bus. Jack would have to keep well away from Brian for the foreseeable future, but he knew deep down this was far from over. Jack Watson just couldn't let it go. He still felt like the victim in all this and it was upsetting him no end. Childhood memories kept taunting him, He was sick and tired of being the victim. Patience was a virtue, and Jack had this in abundance.

CHAPTER 50

Jack brought Jeff along to the craft fair, not that he had much choice in the matter. Jeff had been asking for weeks. It was a bright day and business was good. Young Jeff was a star behind the Watson stall, full of banter. The ladies loved him. The money taken was more than enough to cover all of Jack's overheads and pay Jeff's wages.

The first of the oak kitchens was to be fitted the next day. Jack had subbed this out to a kitchen fitter he had worked with several times. He was by no means cheap but he was a brilliant tradesman who did his job with pride. If he left any snags he would be embarrassed. So,

Jack knew there would be no come backs. This would free up his time to make the second kitchen and get started on the various pieces of furniture on the books. Work was beginning to pile up. Jack needed help and had arranged to interview two joiners the following week. As much as Jack loved being on the tools, he knew he would have to step away in order to progress the business.

By the time Jack dropped jeff off and finished the final preparation for the kitchen back at the workshop, it was nearly half past eight when he got home. The little fella would already be asleep. Jack found this part of running his own business the hardest. He had to sacrifice a lot of time with his son. He knew this was only for the short term.

The house was in darkness as he walked inside, alarm bells began ringing in his head. There was no sign of Laura, he flicked the hall light on and ran upstairs. He was stopped in his tracks by the sight of his wife laying on the floor outside of the bathroom. She was bleeding from her ear and there was a lot of blood on her legs. He called her name but she did not respond. Jacks first aid training kicked in. She wasn't conscious but was breathing. He rolled her gently into the recovery position and dialled 999. He made a second call to Gene; she was quickly becoming hysterical as Jack broke the news. "You have to calm down Gene. I need you to come over. The ambulance is on its way. I need you to look after Robbie." Gene quietened down, "Of course, yes, I'm on my way. Ray will drive me."

Jack sat on the floor and stroked the head of his stricken wife. "I love you Laura." He whispered time and time again. He was praying that Gene got there before the ambulance, he didn't want to leave her side.

It seemed like an age before Jack heard the sirens outside, although it had only been fifteen minutes. He ran down the stairs and let them in, and pointed up to where Laura was prone. He told them she was breathing but not responding he also said her pulse was very rapid. Jack followed them up. One of the paramedics carried out the same response checks that Jack had done. He worked quickly and calmly. He sent the other one to get the stretcher from the ambulance.

"What's happened to her?" Jack pleaded.

"It's too early to tell. We need to get her to the hospital quick smart." He inserted a drip into the back of Lauras hand, explaining it would slow her pulse down. The stretcher was brought up and they asked Jack to give them space.

"Do you need me to help?"

"No sir, go downstairs and keep the front door open."

"Be careful of the baby."

Jack couldn't believe how quickly they had put Laura onto the stretcher and carried her downstairs. He had to admire their professionalism and their calmness. Jack ran upstairs and peeped in on Robbie, he was sleeping soundly. As he got back to the ambulance, Ray's car pulled up and Gene, Ray and Beth all ran out. They all started talking at once, surprisingly Jack was the calmest of the four, the paramedics must have had this effect on him.

"Nothing has changed since I spoke to you on the phone, Robbie is asleep, he didn't hear a thing. I'm going with Laura. I will call you as soon as I know anything." Gene was choking back the tears as she squeezed Jack's hand.

"She will be ok love; she is as tough as old boots;" she said trying to raise a smile.

"Go on son." Ray added.

Beth wanted to go with Jack in the ambulance. The paramedics said no, they needed all the space to treat Laura. Jack jumped in. The lights started flashing and the sirens rang out as they sped away. Gene, Ray and Beth, stood in stunned silence, no one knowing what to say or do.

Beth broke the silence. "Give me your keys dad, I'm going to the hospital, Jack shouldn't be on his own at a time like this." Ray handed them over, without a word. Beth left as Gene and Ray made their way inside to check on the little fella.

As the paramedics pushed Laura's stretcher through the hospital entrance, they were quickly joined by a doctor and two nurses. All Jack could hear was noise as they listed Lauras vital signs. He followed behind, feeling alone, almost as if he didn't exist. He was only allowed to go so far; another nurse stopped him and took him to the family waiting room. She told Jack that a doctor would be along to update him on his wife's condition. The room was empty, now he really was alone. He sat alone, scared and helpless. His mind trying to make sense of what had happened to Laura, had she fainted, or tripped and hit her head? Why was she bleeding from the ear? Had she lost their baby? He held his head in his hands and tried to shake these thoughts. He tried to tell himself that everything was going to be fine.

Jacks thoughts turned to the visit from the police, had this caused her too much stress? He blamed Brian Rice, the anger inside him was so intense he wanted to hurt that prick, like he has never wanted to hurt anyone in the past. The trouble with Jack was that he couldn't see that he was to blame. If he had just let it rest after the first graffiti attack, then none of this would have happened. He just couldn't let it go even if he knew he had cost STG more than they owed him. One thing was for sure, Jack wasn't finished with Brian Rice, not by a long chalk.

He then remembered his previous visits to hospital, only one ended well, the birth of Robbie. One of the happiest days of his life. After his mother had broken the vodka bottle over his head, he was taken into care and life was never the same for him. Then his great mate and new Dad Peter was taken from him. Jacks eyes filled with tears, He wiped them away quickly, he had to stay strong for Laura.

The door to the waiting room opened, Jack was on his feet like a shot, expecting to see a doctor. It was Beth, she ran into his arms and gave him a big hug.

"Any news Jack?"

"No, they have taken her for tests, they just stuck me in here and told me to wait."

Shall I go and see if I can find anything out?"

"No Beth, they said the doctor will come and talk to me as soon as they know what's wrong." They sat down, Beth took Jack's hand,

"She will be ok Jack; she is one tough cookie." She was trying to convince herself as much as Jack. She gave her mum a call with the little news she had and promised to call back when there were some developments.

Two hours passed by, they had chatted a little about this and that, just passing time. Beth reminisced about the wedding day, they both managed to smile for the first time since they arrived. Jack was happy to have Beth there, he needed the company, it was too hard being left on his own, too much time to think and hate. He found it difficult to maintain eye contact with Beth, she was the spitting image of Laura, same hair style, same figure and same taste in clothes. Beth was every bit as beautiful as Laura. Their red hair and the green eyes were so striking they would make any man go weak at the knees.

Jack often teased Ray, saying that his two daughters definitely got their looks from their mother. Gene who was now north of fifty-five, could still turn a few heads.

It was over three hours, now approaching mid-night when the doctor came into the waiting room. It was still only Jack and Beth in the room. Jack was scared.

"Mr Watson, my name is Doctor Yasmin. Your wife is very poorly indeed, it appears she has a bleed on the brain." Again, Jack's mind flashed back to Peter.

"She is now having a brain scan so we will know a bit more after. She is still unconscious and not responsive. Her heart rate is fast and her breathing is stable."

"What about the baby?"

"The baby is fine; we have a good strong heartbeat. We are monitoring both your wife and your child. If the baby shows any signs of stress, we will need to carry out a caesarean section. We need you to sign a consent form to allow us to proceed if necessary. Believe me Mr Watson this will only be done as a last resort."

"Of course, I will sign. How long until we know the result of the scan?"

"It will be a few hours Mr Watson, we are doing everything we can. I will come back as soon as I know more." Jack thanked him as he left. Beth and Jack stood there unable to find any words. Beth, left to call her parents with the update. Gene was close to hysterical. She wanted to come to the hospital. Beth managed to calm her down, explaining there was no point, as no one was allowed to see Laura yet.

CHAPTER 51

It was nearer to three hours when Doctor Jasmine came back into the waiting room. Beth had fallen asleep around an hour ago, she was roused by the doctors voice.

"Mr Watson, Laura has a swelling of her brain, we have had to put her into an induced coma. Jack was stunned. "What? Why? I don't understand."

Laura's heart is beating far too rapidly, sending too much blood to the brain. This is causing the swelling to worsen. This is a normal reaction in such cases. Putting her into a coma will allow us to slow this down. Her heartbeat is now normal and her breathing is stable. She is in an intensive care unit, where she will be monitored twenty-four seven. We are also monitoring your babies heartbeat, which at the moment is strong and constant. We have attached a drip to Laura which will provide enough energy for both her and the baby. If the baby shows any signs of stress, we need to perform a caesarean section, to avoid any stress to Laura."

Jack was struggling to take it all in.

"I need you to sign the consent form to allow us to do this, I can assure you it will only be done as a last resort." Dr Jasmine repeated his earlier message.

"Of course, I will sign," he said taking the papers from the doctor.

"What caused this to happen?"

"At the moment we are not sure, it is possible that Laura fainted and hit her head. There is no sign of bruising, but this is the most likely cause. The good news is there are no tumour's and we have stopped the bleeding.

Beth spoke for the first time since waking.

"How long will she be in a coma?"

"It varies from patient to patient, some a matter of weeks, others a matter of months. It depends how quickly the swelling reduces. We will only keep Laura in the coma as long as is absolutely necessary."

"Can we see her?" Jack and Beth said, almost at the same time.

"As I said Laura is in intensive care. Only medical staff are allowed into the room. You can see her through the glass, but only for a few minutes."

"I should be with her, she's my wife."

"Mr Watson, I understand that this is difficult for you, but believe me when I tell you, Laura needs complete rest. Even though she is in a coma, there is a risk that she might recognise your voice or become aware of your smell. This could cause her to fight to regain consciousness, it's a human reaction. This could be fatal." The Doctors words were sobering to both Jack and Beth.

As they looked through the glass it was easy to tell it was Laura. Most of her face was covered by an oxygen mask and there were tubes everywhere. The flaming red hair was a giveaway. Jack's heart ached, he again felt helpless, useless even. How he wished he could hold her hand. How he wished he could see her beautiful eyes. The pain he felt was alien to him. A nurse came over and told them it was time to go. Jack was now crying shamelessly. "I need to stay here; I should be with my wife when she wakes up." The nurse put her hand on Jack's shoulder.

"You need to go home and rest, your wife will need you to be strong, she will need a lot of help when she comes home," The word when and not if, resonated with Jack, he felt his pain ease.

"We will give you plenty of notice when we are going to bring Laura out of the coma Mr Watson. You can come back for a few minutes each day." Jack put his face close to the glass and mouthed the words. "Sweet dreams my darling, I love you. See you tomorrow."

He blew two kisses, one to his wife, the other to his unborn child.

Beth linked Jack's arm and said. "Come on mister, I'll drive you home."

Gene and Ray were both awake when they got to the house. Jack was relieved that Beth filled them in on all the developments. Robbie had slept through all the drama, peacefully unaware. Jack went up and sat with him for a while, just watching his son. Happy in the land of nod. When he got back downstairs, Beth was curled up asleep on the settee. Ray went to wake her, Jack said, "Let her sleep Mate, she is shattered. I'll get a blanket and pillow."

Gene gave Jack a big hug and told him to stay strong. Ray shook his hand and patted him on the back, he couldn't find any words to say. Jack understood.
Once they had left, Jack kissed Beth on the forehead and went to bed. Day

break was beginning, sleep came quicker than he expected. The nurses words, "when she comes home," had given him more comfort than he first thought.

CHAPTER 52

When Jack woke and went into Robbie's room, his little bed was empty. Then he heard Beth, chatting away downstairs. As he walked in the kitchen the little fellas eyes widened with delight. "Daddy, Daddy," he called arms stretched out. "Hello Robbie, how's my little soldier? Is Aunty Beth looking after you?" Robbie smiled and nodded.

"Of course, his aunty is looking after him, I have told him that his mum is staying at our parents' house for a few days, resting. And I will be looking after him for a while." Jack was a bit shocked. "Oh OK, but what about work?" Jack knew that Beth had been temping for a while, not sure on a career path.

"I have nothing on this week, I really would like to help."

"I appreciate it Beth, but I will pay you whatever your hourly rate is."

"Don't be silly Jack, I don't want paying. Robbie is my nephew for goodness sake."

"Thanks Beth, but I can manage."

"What are you talking about Jack?" You have a business to run."

"I can't focus on work, with Laura laying in a bloody coma."

"Jack, how do you think Laura would feel if she thought you were moping around, feeling sorry for yourself?" Jack knew this made sense. "Thanks Beth, but only if you agree to earning a few quid."

"We can discuss that later; now go and have a shower you look as rough as a badger."

"Thanks sis." Jack said with a smile.

As he showered, he knew Beth was right, he needed to keep the business running, as difficult as it was. It would be far better than sitting around the house all day worrying. And he could teach that cunt Rice, a lesson he wouldn't forget in a hurry.

Before Jack left to go to his workshop, he put Beth on the car insurance, so she could get around, Take Robbie to see nan and grandad and do a bit of shopping, there was sod all in the fridge, He gave her his credit card.

At the warehouse, Jack saw in his diary, today was when he was to interview two joiners, he didn't feel up to it, however now he needed help more than ever. Jeff gave his best wishes for Laura and went about his tasks.

Jack started making the units for the next oak kitchen, he reasoned that if he had one made before the interviews, he could use it as a benchmark. The first to

turn up was Billy, quite a bit older than Jack, very smartly turned out in a fetching blue suit, he looked in good shape for his age, strong and fit. Jack liked the bloke from the outset, he had an impressive resume. and had worked on many high-end products. After a quick chat about wages, Jack asked him when he could start. "Tomorrow"
"Brilliant, see you at eight."

The second candidate was around Jack's age, very muscular, with a mop of curly ginger hair. Jack thought, he must be Irish. "Hi I'm Michael, Michael o' Flannagan." Jack held back a smile. Michael was in his work attire; he had brought an impressive looking toolbox with him. "This is an example of my work Mr Watson, I really need this job, I have a baby on the way. I can start straight away."
"Ok, slow down a minute," Jack smiled, holding his hand up.

"I'll tell you what, if you can make a base unit, the same as this one, the job is yours."

"No bother at all Mr Watson." Michael said, his big smile showing off a fine set of white teeth.

Michael made the unit with little fuss, and every bit as quickly and as good as Jack. "The jobs yours, see you tomorrow at eight, and don't worry I'll pay you for what you have done today."

"Jesus, thanks Mr Watson."

"Call me Jack."

"Yes Sir Mr, er I mean Jack." Both men laughed.

Jack spent the rest of the day doing the paperwork. He was grateful to Beth for giving him a kick up the arse that morning.

Jack was only allowed to see Laura for five minutes; she was in exactly the same position as the day before. The nurse told him that both mother and child were stable, another scan was due the following morning to see how the swelling was responding. She told Jack to come in at Two o' clock the next day to see Doctor Jasmine.

Jack called Beth to see if she fancied fish and chips. She said that she had cooked spaghetti bolognaise and it would be ready when he got home. Jack thanked her and rang off. He then gave Gene a quick call to keep her informed, he knew she was as worried as him.

After dinner, Beth asked if it was alright if she stayed in the spare room, as it would be easier than driving back and forth, Jack agreed, it made sense.

CHAPTER 53

Laura had been in the induced coma for almost a week. Doctor Jasmine was very positive about her progress. Two scans had shown a significant reduction in the swelling on her brain. He told Jack, that if she continued to recover at this rate, they would bring her out of the coma sooner, rather than later. He also advised Jack that he thought the safest option would be to deliver the baby by caesarean section before they woke Laura. The concern was that the rigours of childbirth could be too much for Laura. He told Jack to think about it. Jack said he would talk it over with Laura's parents.

Beth was doing a wonderful job looking after little Robbie, the house was spotless and she was a great cook, she also did the washing and ironing. Beth was certainly enjoying her role as a surrogate mother and wife.

Jacks new employees had hit the ground running, both were exceptionally talented joiners. Michael was making the kitchen units at a fair rate of knots. Billy was working on two bespoke Welsh dressers; He was ahead of Jack's schedule. Jack knew well he was very lucky to find these two. Along with Jeff, who flitted between helping both Billy and Michael. A bigger bonus was that all three got along and worked well together. During one lunch break, Billy suggested, that if Jack bought another bench saw and router, production could be speeded up. There was enough cash in the bank, so no need to take up the banks offer of a top up loan. The order book was full for the next three months, so it made sense to expand. Jack also decided to lease another van, Michael was keen to do the craft fairs, Jack thought with his Irish charm and winning smile, he would be a great success, along with Jeff.

Jack asked Beth if she minded looking after Robbie on a Saturday, as he needed to go and see some potential clients. She was only too happy to help. Jack had a couple of appointments, but his real reason for asking Beth, was that he was planning a visit to his old nemesis, Brian Rice.

CHAPTER 54

Jack parked his car a few doors down from Brian's house, on the opposite side of the road. Through the scope on his rifle, he could see Rice's car, now he just needed to sit and wait for his prey to appear. This was the final act for Jack, after this he would let it go, and forget about that prick, once and for all. He intended to make this a very painful final lesson for dear old Brian. Jack had brought both his rifles, one loaded with pellets and the other with a single dart. He knew he wouldn't have time to mess about reloading. He kept the gun trained on the target. As he sat humming, and tapping his fingers on the steering wheel, there he was, the man himself. Smartly dressed as always, sporting a well fitted blue suit and a red tie.

The first shot hit Brian on his right shin, quickly followed by a second which smashed into the other shin. Brian was on the floor clutching both legs. Anyone who has ever played football, cricket or hockey, would be fully aware of the agony felt from a shin injury. Time for rifle number two.

As Jack lined up his third shot, Brian staggered to his feet and was joined by Mrs Rice, she was trying to get him back into the house. Jack aimed at Brians shoulder; his target was the collar bone. He wanted him to remember this day for the rest of his life. As Jack squeezed the trigger his arm slipped causing the front of the rifle to rise. The dart hit Brian, Jack heard him cry out and saw him fall back to the ground. Mrs Rice let out a deafening scream, Time to get out of here Jack thought. He sped away past his fallen victim. He could see a few neighbours gathering, none looked at the car as he drove away. Jack was well pleased with himself, finally I can forget about that fucking horrible little shit, he told himself. Jack then went about his business, he had two house calls to make, hopefully more orders for his rapidly expanding company.

The Dart missed Jack's intended target, It was embedded into Brian's temple, he was unconscious, blood pouring from the wound. Mrs Rice was completely hysterical, sobbing, calling out her husband's name, over and over. One of her neighbours had called for an ambulance another had turned Brian into the recovery position, and gently laid a towel over the dart in an attempt to stem the blood flow.

Jack got home around three o' clock. Beth had again surpassed herself in the kitchen, one of Jack's favourites, rib eye steak, Jacket potato, mushrooms and onions and of course marrow fat peas. "I'm going to miss you when you go Beth, you spoil me rotten."

"Well, you are my brother-in-law, it's the least I can do for Laura."

After Beth had left, Jack took Robbie to the park, his favourite was the swings, he loved it when Jack pushed him high. Jack brought some bird seed to feed the ducks. It was so comical watching Robbie chasing the ducks. He loved spending time with his son, how he wished that Laura was by his side. The little fella had asked when will he see mummy? "Soon mate, very soon."

Back at home once Robbie was tucked up in bed, Jack read him a story, after ten minutes the little mite was in a deep sleep. Beth had certainly been keeping him active that was for sure.

Downstairs, Jack flicked the telly on and grabbed a cold beer from the fridge, He would only have one, in case the hospital called.

He had spoken with Gene and Ray about what Doctor Jasmine had advised about the baby, all three thought it was the best option. Jack stretched out on his leather recliner. The headline on the London news, caused his mouth to drop open. A reporter was in the street where Brian Rice lived, police had taped off access and there were a lot of police cars everywhere. A large crowd had also gathered. "Fuck thought Jack, this doesn't look good." He was now sat up and listened intently to the reporter.

"Today at around twelve o' clock, a man in his early fifties was shot three times, with what the police believe to be a high-powered air rifle. He was hit in both legs by pellets and a third shot, which was an arrow or dart, hit the victim in the temple. The news from the hospital is that the victim is in a critical condition, having suffered a cardiac arrest in the ambulance. Police have been knocking door to door to see if anyone has any information. The police also added that a grey car, possibly a Ford was seen speeding down this very road just after the incident."

Jack was shocked, he had intended to teach Rice a lesson, but not this, he hoped he would be alright. He had to think, and quickly. He needed to get rid of his rifles and all the pellets and darts. He brought the guns into the house and cleaned them so there was no prints. He planned to dump them in the river Lea on his way to the hospital the next day. Jack knew that Brian, and or his wife would put his name in the frame, especially after their altercation in the pub. He needed to stay calm, they couldn't prove anything, nobody saw him and his car is a Ford, black not grey. Nonetheless Jack fully expected to get a visit from the boys in blue. He hoped that if and when they come banging on his door, it would be before Laura was home. He knew she would go ballistic. Jack could handle a rollocking but he didn't want to cause Laura any unnecessary stress while she is recuperating. "What have you done Jack?" was the question going over and over in his head.

CHAPTER 55

After Jack had dropped Robbie off at his grandparents, he headed for the hospital. Doctor Jasmine saw him straight away; Jack told him that if the safest option was to deliver the baby while Laura was still in a coma then he could go ahead. The doctor explained that the rate the swelling was decreasing had slowed, the good news was that Laura was responding to the treatment, but it could be necessary to keep her under, for at least another two to four weeks.

"When will you do the Caesarion?"

"There is no rush Mr Watson, the babies due date is in a week. We will wait until then."

Jack went to see Laura, again only through the glass window. She was still in the same position; his heart was breaking every time he saw her like this. But he knew she was in good hands and was getting the best treatment possible. The NHS do a remarkable job all things considered. She was improving all the time, Jack wondered what, if anything Laura would remember. The doctor hadn't talked about what condition she will be in when they wake her up. That was a conversation for another day.

As Jack was walking out, he was gobsmacked to see Brian Rice's wife walking in. She recognised him straight away.

"What are you doing here, you bastard. Have you come to finish the job?"

"What are you talking about woman? Who the hell are you?"

"Don't give me that shit. You know well who I am. This mad bastard shot my husband." She yelled pointing at

Jack, People were staring, a nurse came over and tried to calm Mrs Rice down.

"The woman's deluded," Jack said as he headed for the exit.

"They will lock you up for this you mad bastard." Jack couldn't believe the timing. He hadn't considered the fact that Brian would be in the same hospital as Laura. It should have occurred to him. Now he had to try and avoid bumping into Mrs Rice each time he comes. He wondered how Brian was doing, he couldn't ask though. That would only arouse suspicion.

Mrs Rice, stood by her husbands bed, stroking his hand and sobbing quietly. The consultant told her that Brian was very poorly indeed, the next twenty-four hours would be critical. She asked him if her husband was going to die? He answered that they were doing all they can. Mrs Rice, loved Brian, for all his faults. Yes, he could be a cantankerous old git. But he was her old git, they had been together since they were sixteen. She stroked his head. "Come back to me Brian, I love you as I did when we met, I need you darling. Be strong I will see you tomorrow." Mrs Rice was a broken woman.

The light was beginning to fade, so Jack headed down to the river Lee. It was always quiet in the early evening. He walked deep into the forest, went to one of the many little jetties in place for fishermen. Jack had put all the tins of pellets and darts into the case with the rifles. This would ensure it would sink to the bottom and hopefully never be recovered. A final look around, all was clear. Jack threw the case with all his might, It was heavy and he only managed to launch it about twelve feet, he watched as it sank as soon as it hit the water. Jack waited there for a good twenty minutes, making sure it didn't resurface. He had no idea what he would have done if it had. When he was satisfied Jack, drove to pick up

Robbie and Beth. On route he thought about his alibi for the time of the shooting, could he asked Beth to lie for him and say he didn't leave the house until mid-day on Saturday? This would make her suspicious, even though she wasn't aware of his run ins with Brian Rice, she would be curious to know why he wanted her to lie. Would she tell Laura? Jack couldn't take the chance. He needed to be smarter.

When Beth and little Robbie were in the car, Jack asked Beth.

"You don't happen to remember what time I left on Saturday do you Beth?"

"I haven't got a clue Jack; Robbie can be very demanding and I seldom have time to look at my watch. The day just flies when I'm with him. That's a strange question, is it important?"

"Not really. I keep a diary of anything work related, Laura does the accounts and she is very meticulous. She likes to put a cost to every minute I am working. Even though it is our business I still need to be paid a salary.

"Sorry Jack, I can't help you there". Jack tapped the steering wheel, "No problem, I remember, football focus had just started before I left. So, it must have been shortly after twelve." He hoped this would register sub-consciously with Beth. The attack on Brian was at twelve o'clock, no man can be two places at the same time. Jack was feeling quite smug with himself.

"There you go then, problem sorted." Beth said feigning interest, while singing with Robbie.

CHAPTER 56

Detective inspector Lock headed the investigation into the shooting of Brian Rice. He was a bit put out at first, questioning why a man of his experience was given such a minor case. Over thirty years' service in which he had headed, and indeed solved some of London's major crimes. He kept in good shape and retirement was looming large, he couldn't wait. He enjoyed his job for the most part but now he had had his fill. He took pride in his appearance always in a suit and tie. He had more hair on his chin than on his head. His wife was always on to him to shave the little that was left. He was to be assisted by detective constable Blackwood. Thirty-five years younger than Lock, he was full of enthusiasm, no matter what the case was. Blackwood had only been in CID for the past two years having been promoted from uniform. Lock thought he was destined for the top; he had all the makings of a fine detective. Not only was he very intelligent, he was also very diligent and worked in a logical manner, which was how Lock had taught him. Blackwood was also dashingly handsome with well-kept jet-black hair. Young Blackwood had no trouble attracting the fairer sex, colleagues wondered why he was single. What they didn't know was that DC Blackwood was gay, even in this day and age he didn't feel comfortable coming out. After they had interviewed Mrs Rice, who had been adamant it is was a man called Jack Watson that had carried out the attack, They delved deeper into the afore mentioned Mr Watson. Neither had heard of him, but it didn't take long to find out he was known to the police. He had spent time in prison when he was younger. More interesting was recent events where he had been accused of various attacks on ex-employees of a company called STG. Also, he had been accused of causing substantial damage to the properties of, a Steve Ginn and a Brian Rice. These incidents were dealt with by uniform, and it appeared, Jack Watson had alibis for all the offences. DS Lock thought, although he had alibis, it doesn't mean that he wasn't somehow connected with the offences. He told Blackwood to pay a visit to the offices of STG and see what he could glean. Certainly, Steve Ginn would be of interest.

"Let's get a bit of background into the history of this ongoing feud, before we pay Watson a visit."

Mrs Rice had told the detectives how she inadvertently bumped into Watson whilst going to visit her husband in hospital.

"Why was he there? No doubt just to gloat, admire his handy work. He needs to be stopped. This is the second time he has shot my husband; The first time was comparatively minor. Brian was shot in the calf and Steve Ginn was shot in the arse." DS Lock suppressed a smile.

"All this over some stupid dispute about pay."

DC Blackwood, found out why Watson was at the hospital.

"His misses is in a coma boss, and she is almost ready to drop a baby."

"An unlikely coincidence, but a coincidence all the same." He told Blackwood to check in with the hospital periodically. At the moment this is just an assault, grievous bodily harm at best. However, it could easily escalate into a murder inquiry. The consultant didn't hold much hope of Brian Rice making it through the night. As he has already had three cardiac arrests since the shooting, one more and it would be goodnight Vienna.

CHAPTER 57

DC Blackwood spent most of the morning conducting interviews at the offices of STG. First in was Julian Hajar. He spoke mainly well about Jack Watson, saying how good he was at his job. He also spoke of the conflict between Jack and Brian. "They just couldn't stand each other, when they were in the same room the tension was unbearable. Brian used his senior position to keep Jack on his toes."

"What about the assault on you Julian?"

"They never caught anyone for it, Jack was suspected but he had an alibi, if it wasn't him, then I'm sure he arranged it. He sent many emails threatening to make us pay for what he called stealing from him."

"And did STG. steal from him?"

"No, Brian spied on him during his notice period, logging where he was each day. STG paid him according to Brian's report."

"Nothing else has happened to you or your property since the assault?"

"No, I was there when someone," Julian gave the inverted comma sign. "Took a shot at Steve and Brian, funny you never caught anyone for that either."

"That's all, thank you Jullian. Send in Steve Ginn." Steve, shuffled in nervously, he looked guilty even though he wasn't being investigated. Steve reiterated what Jullian had said about the animosity between Brian and Jack. He went as far as to say they hated each other. "Brian wanted him out, and eventually he got his way. I told our MD it was lucky Jack didn't come after STG for constructive dismissal."

"So, Steve, Jack considered his pay to be short to the tune of over two and a half grand, what happened after he left?"

"Jack made all kinds of threats via email. Basically, saying he would get his money back by hook or by crook. He took STG to a wages tribunal but didn't bother to show up. He knew he couldn't win. Brian got a proper rollocking from Adam, our MD. He suggested that Brian should resign over his handling of the Watson saga. It ended up costing the company far more than they hadn't paid Jack."

"What has happened to you personally, since Watson left?"

"The front of my house was covered in graffiti twice and I was shot in the arse by a pellet."

"And you reported these to the police?"

"Yes of course."

"And who do you think was responsible?"

"I told the police then, that of course it was done or arranged by Jack Watson.

I don't know how much of an investigation ensued, but no charges were made."

"Have you seen or spoken to Jack Watson since he left STG?" Steve was quiet for a few moments, unsure whether or not to mention his pay off. He thought it was better to tell the truth.

"yes, I have seen him a few times now, we are members of the same golf club."

"And have you spoken?"

"Yes, I offered to pay him the money he thought he was owed, if he put a stop to the attacks on my property."

"How did Watson react?"

"He said, he had no idea what I was talking about. He was smiling as he said it."

"And then?"

Watson told me if I paid half of the money, he would say no more about the incident. I agreed, I didn't want any embarrassing confrontations at the club. I knew about Watson's visit to the pub to confront Brian."

"So, you paid him off?"

"Yes, the following week at the club. I gave him twelve hundred and fifty pounds. Watson said, Rice was responsible for the rest of the debt. Then we shook hands and that was that." DC Blackwood asked about the character of Brian Rice, was he popular? did he have many enemies? Steve laughed at this.

"Jack Watson is one of a number of enemies Brian has, it is safe to say he is the most unpopular man at the company."

"Thank you Steve, that will be all for now."

Other members of STG, including Barry, who mentioned the incident with his motorbike, John, Mr Partridge in a pear tree and the MD Adam, all confirmed Brian Rice's unpopularity.

DC Blackwood's answered a call from DI Lock.

"Brian Rice didn't make it through the night. We have a murder enquiry on our hands. Come back to the station and we can collate all the information we have before we talk to Watson."

"Yes sir, We may need to talk to several others. It appears the deceased had numerous enemies. I'll be about an hour." DC Blackwood ended the call, and after grabbing a meal deal from Tesco, headed back to the station.

CHAPTER 58

Jack hardly slept the previous evening; he saw the news that his old nemesis was dead. He had killed a man. It didn't matter that is was unintentional, Rice was dead and Jack had killed him. Fuck, what was he to do? Try to stay calm, he told himself. They can't prove anything, can they? Deny everything. Jack was glad he got rid of the guns, at least they won't find the weapons.

As much as Jack hated Brian Rice, he didn't want this, no, even if he was a prick he didn't deserve to die like that. He felt sympathy for Rice's wife and family. Jack had his own family to think about. What would Laura do if he is arrested? He tried to shake that thought as quickly as it arrived.

When he got to the workshop, the boys were having their break. Jeff was reading the Sun newspaper. The first thing Jack saw, was a picture of Brian Rice, staring at him. The bold headline read, "MURDERED ON HIS OWN DOORSTEP." Jack felt sick.

"Top of the morning boss," A cheery Michael greeted him. "Jesus, you look rough, have you been to bed at all?"

"Well thanks Michael, it's very hard to sleep, when my wife is laying in a coma, not knowing if she will live or die." Jack immediately regretted this rebuke.

"I'm sorry boss, take no notice of me, I didn't think."

"No, I'm sorry Michael, I'm a bit cranky this morning. You didn't deserve that."

"No worries boss, I understand." Jeff looked up from the newspaper and said, "Isn't this the bloke you used to work with?" He said pointing to the front page. Jack puffed out his cheeks.

"Yes, it's a bit of a surprise. Truth is he was a horrible bully of a man. I doubt he will be mourned by many." Jack walked into his office. The three boys looked at each other in silent shock. Michael whispered, "I thought you wasn't supposed to speak ill of the dead?"

Jack sat alone with his thoughts. He knew his alibi for the day of the shooting was not strong. Beth was the only one who saw him that morning. He tried to think, had he stopped anywhere on the way to Rice's house? Did he go to a shop or get fuel. These places would have CCTV. His head was frazzled, he couldn't remember clearly. He was pretty sure he had made no stops.

The worst thing now was the waiting. He knew the boys in blue were coming, but when? His mobile rang, it was The hospital. A nurse spoke very calmly, she told Jack that there had been some complications and Doctor Jasmine has decided to deliver the baby this morning. Laura was being prepared for surgery. Jack let out a cry of anguish, "God no." He hung up and rushed out of the workshop without a word to the boys. Once again, they were left with nothing to say, all they could do was shrug their shoulders.

CHAPTER 59

An incident room was set up at Hertford police station. DI Lock had been allocated more resources, given the seriousness of the case. Along with DC Blackwood, sitting in the room were four young DC's. Jon Wright, Sara Gower, Nick Jones and IT wizard Grace Williams. All sat there open eyed with notebooks and pens at the ready. DI Lock began.

"You have all been briefed as to the events leading up to the death of Brian Rice. We are led to believe Rice, was not a popular man and over many years had gained more enemies than friends." Lock walked over to a big white board positioned at the front of the room. "We have a few suspects; one stands out in particular. This one, Jack Watson. He is known to the police and has been a resident in her majesty's establishments, both borstal and mainline prison. His wife is pregnant, she is in intensive care in a coma, maybe this pushed him over the edge. He has a motive. DC Blackwood and I will bring him in for questioning. Wright and Gower, I need you two to do some digging into his past, find out what you can about his interests. Talk to his employees, he owns a furniture making company called Watson and family Ltd. See if he has been acting strangely since the shooting of Rice. See if you can find anything related to air rifle shooting. Williams and Jones, I need you to go to STG offices and take statements from all employees. DC Blackwood has already had quite useful informal chats, with a few of the directors. Find out about the feud between Watson and Rice, Get names of others with grudges against Rice.

Although I am almost positive that Watson is our man, we need to keep our options open. We will have another sit down in three days; once we have spoken with Watson." The four young detectives started chatting amongst themselves. "Come on, look lively," Said an irritated looking DI Lock. "There is no time to sit around gossiping, get out there and start asking questions. That's what we, the police are supposed to do isn't it?" One of them said "Yes sir." As they hurried away.

"Come on then Blackwood, let's go visit Mr Watson for a friendly little chat." Blackwood had been in many friendly little chats involving DI Lock, Friendly wasn't the first word that sprung to mind. Lock was DI for a reason. He was bloody good.

CHAPTER 60

Jack had got to the hospital in record time. There was no news as yet, Laura was still in surgery. Once again Jack found himself alone in the family waiting room. Gene and Ray arrived a short time later. "Any news?" Asked a concerned looking Ray. Gene's eyes were red from the tears that had already fallen. "Nothing yet, it shouldn't be too much longer now." Jack held Gene in a tight embrace. Ray told Jack that he looked exhausted. If only he knew what else Jack had to worry about, he would understand why. There was no two ways about it, Jack Watson was in a real mess. Doctor Jasmine came in, all three jumped to their feet in expectation, each one too scared to speak.

"Mr Watson, you have a fine healthy baby girl," Jack fell back on to his chair, he couldn't hold back the tears a moment longer, he tried to speak but words failed him.

"How is Laura?" asked Ray, trying to remain calm. "Your daughter is a very strong young woman; she took the operation very well. We are very hopeful we can wake her in a couple of days.

Jack found it hard to believe the words. He managed to blub thank you doctor through his sobs.

"Would you like to spend a few minutes with your daughter Mr Watson?" Doctor Jasmine knew the answer before he asked the question.

Jack marvelled at the little miracle in his palm, she had a small whisp of reddish hair, her tiny hands and feet were purple. It looked like she was wearing gloves and socks. After a few minutes, the nurse took the baby and Jack watched through the window as she put his little princess into an incubator by the side of Laura's bed. He looked at his wife with a love stronger than ever. She had fewer tubes now that the baby was born. It may have been Jack's imagination but he thought she was looking better. "I love you Laura," he shouted more loudly than he intended. "You did it darling, soon we will all be home." Ray offered to drive Jack home but he insisted he was fine. He looked like a different man from the one that came to the hospital. Half of the stress had left him and it showed on his face.

Beth came running down the hall to greet him when he got home. Gene had phoned her with the news. "Oh Jack, It's wonderful, you must be the happiest man alive?" They embraced for what Jack felt was for too long. Beth nestled her face into Jacks chest. Then reached up and kissed him softly on the cheek. Jack felt a stirring in his groin and pulled away from the embrace, hoping that Beth didn't feel it.

"Are we having a drink to celebrate?" She asked smiling. If she had felt something, Jack thought she was a bloody good actress.

"No Beth, we should wait until Laura is awake then we can smash it." Jack said miming knocking back a glass of booze.

"Fair enough, tea or coffee then?" Before Jack could answer, there was a loud knock at the door. He turned in shock and saw two burley shadows through the glass. He knew who had come to call, he had been expecting them for a while.

CHAPTER 61

"Mr Jack Watson?"

"Yes, that's me."

"I am Detective inspector Lock, and this is DC Blackwood," both men showed their badges. Jack barely glanced at them.

"Can we come in?"

"What is this about?"

"It would be better inside sir, or you can come down to the station if you would prefer?"

"No, come in." Jack showed them through into the front room and offered them a seat. Beth stood there looking completely baffled. "Would you like some tea or coffee?" Jack cut her an old-fashioned look, which told her, that was the wrong thing to say. "For fuck sake Beth, what do you think this is, a fucking tea party? Why don't you make them a fucking cheese sandwich too while you're at it?" DI Lock politely declined, and Beth left, fighting back the tears. She wondered how Jack could have spoken to her like that in front of people, after all she had done for him. Only a few minutes earlier she had felt his manhood growing as they embraced. It seemed to Beth that Jack wanted her as much as she wanted him.

DI Lock began. "It appears you are not too keen on the police Jack."
"What do you expect? Your lot tried to stitch me up on an assault charge. How can I trust you?"
"We are not here to discuss that Jack. I think you know the reason for our visit. Jack, I can call you Jack?" Jack remained silent. "I take it you have heard about the death of Brian Rice?"
"Yes, I saw it on the news."

"You didn't like him very much, did you Jack?"

"That's a bit of an understatement, I couldn't stand the man,"

"Did you have anything to do with the shooting Jack?"

"No, as much as I despised the man, I wouldn't want him dead." DC Blackwood spoke. "Perhaps you didn't mean to kill him, just cause him some pain. Teach him a lesson, so to speak?"

"I had nothing to do with it." DI Lock took the lead again. "Do you own an air rifle Jack?"

"No."

"Have you ever owned an air rifle Jack?"

"Yes, but that was many years ago, before I was married. I had a couple of guns."

"What happened to the guns Jack?"

"I sold them to some bloke down the pub."

"I don't suppose he has a name?"

" Bloody hell, I can't remember."

"What were your movements on the morning and afternoon on the twelfth of May?" Jack squinted his eyes as if trying to remember. "Come on Jack, It's only a couple of weeks ago."

"I was home all morning. In the afternoon I went to see a couple of potential clients."

"Can anyone verify this?"

"Beth, my wife's sister, who you just met was here looking after my son. I can give you the names and addresses of the clients."

"What time did you leave the house?" Jack again put on his thinking face. He picked up his diary from the coffee table. "There it is, I left just after twelve."

"You keep a diary of your movements? That's a bit unusual."

"It's for my wife, she does the accounts and wants me to log all my working hours. Here see for yourself." Jack handed the diary to DC Blackwood, who flicked through it. "It's pretty comprehensive guv." He made a note of the two names and addresses for the clients Jack had claimed to have seen.

"Ok Jack. That will do for now. While I'm here I might as well have a word with Beth." Jack tried to hide the look of alarm on his face. Too Late, DI Lock spotted it straight away.

"Jack opened the door and called out, "Beth can you come here please? They want to have a word with you."

"Me, why, what have I done?" She said as she walked into the front room." Jack left them to it. DC Blackwood asked Beth to sit down. "So, Beth, you are Laura's sister? How is she by the way?"

"She is still in a coma but doing well. Today she gave birth to a little girl. We are so happy."

"That's great news. This won't take long. Do you live here Beth?"

"No, I have been looking after my nephew Robbie since Laura has been in the hospital. I stay here Monday to Friday. Jack has Robbie on the weekends."

"But you were here on Saturday the twelfth of May, is that correct?"

"Yes, Jack asked me to come over as he had to go to work."

"Can you remember what time Jack left?"

"Yeah sure, it was just after twelve."

"You seem pretty certain of that Beth?"

"I am, He told me he left after the start of some football show on the telly, which started at twelve."

"Wait a minute Beth. Jack told you he left after twelve, Is that correct?"

"Yes, that's what I just said wasn't it?"

"We need to know what time you remember Jack leaving, not what time he told you he left. This is very important Beth."

"I haven't got a clue; little Robbie keeps me so busy; I never have an idea of the time. But if Jack said it was after twelve, then it was after twelve."

"Thanks Beth that will be all. We will be on our way." Jack opened the door to let them out.

"We will be speaking to you again shortly Mr Watson. Don't leave the country." Jack slammed the door behind them, without uttering a word.

Jack joined Beth in the kitchen. She was still in shock from his earlier outburst.

"How could you talk to me like that Jack? After all I have done for you. You made me feel so small."

"I'm sorry Beth. You didn't deserve that; it is so unlike me. With all that's happening with Laura I'm so stressed. Not sleeping well or eating properly. The last thing I need is the police poking around. It's no excuse, I shouldn't have treated you like that. I really am sorry Beth. I appreciate all you have done, more than I can ever say. Come here and give me a hug." Beth nestled into Jack and he held her in a tight embrace. Jack could feel his manhood starting to grow. Beth felt it hardening against her tummy. Jack broke away from the embrace, the bulge in his trousers was evident. He sat on a stool in an attempt to hide it. Beth didn't comment.

"What did the police ask you?" Jack said trying to ease the situation.

"They wanted to know what time you left on the Saturday that bloke was shot."

"What did you tell them Beth?"

"I told them what you said. You left shortly after twelve o' clock."

"Did they believe you?"

"I have no idea, Jack. It's a bit of a coincidence, you asking me that same question about the time you left." Beth was many things but stupid wasn't one of them.

"I have done nothing wrong Beth; You have to believe me. Hopefully, this will all of died down before Laura comes home. I don't want to cause her any stress or upset. Beth had a bad feeling that Jack was lying.

"I won't say anything to Laura, but one thing is for sure, she will find out sooner or later."

"The later the better." Jack replied with eyebrow's raised.

CHAPTER 62

Jack kept pacing up and down in the family waiting room at the hospital. Laura's parent's sat in anxious silence. Beth was looking after Robbie at home. Two hours earlier, Laura had been woken from her coma and was now undergoing an assessment as to her condition. Jack was about to go and see if he could get any update, when a smiling Doctor Jasmine entered the room. All three looked at him in anticipation.

"Laura has come through her ordeal remarkably well. The swelling has completely disappeared and she has no sign of any brain damage. She is obviously confused and tired. We have explained all to her and she has spent a short time holding your daughter. She asked to see her handsome man, I assume that is you, Mr Watson?" Doctor Jasmine said smiling even wider.

"Can we go in?" Jack asked with tears of joy forming in his eyes.

"Only you Mr Watson, and only for five minutes." He turned to face Laura's parents.

"You can see your daughter through the glass if you like?"

Laura greeted Jack with a tired smile, there was no mistaking the love for her husband in those beautiful green eyes.

"I love you my handsome man." She said, offering Jack her hand.

"I love you too darling. I have missed you so much. You gave us quite a scare. Your mum said you were as tough as old boots, and she was right." Laura glanced up to look at her parent's both crying tears of unbridled joy, waving and blowing kisses.

Jack picked up their daughter and said.

"You have met our beautiful princess? She will be a heartbreaker just like her mother." Laura smiled again.

"You have always been a charmer Mr Watson. I would like to call her Rosie. What do you think?"

"I love it. Robbie and Rosie. Perfect."

"How is the little fella?"

"He is fine. Beth has been an absolute star, looking after him so I could keep the business running." They were interrupted by a nurse saying that was enough for one day. Jack kissed her very gently on the lips and the love he felt for Laura was stronger than ever. Outside the room, Jack asked Doctor Jasmine what happened next? He explained. "Laura will need physio for the next week to get her strength back. We will do a scan every two days. If all goes well, as I expect it will, your family will be home in seven days." Jack took him by the hand and squeezed it hard, "Thank you so much Doctor Jasmine, for everything." Tears flowing down

Jack's cheeks just as freely as Laura's parents.

CHAPTER 63

DI Lock called the incident room at Hertford police station to order. He commanded great respect and the room fell silent within seconds.

"Ok, what did we find out at STG? Did anyone else have as bigger a grudge against Rice, than our main suspect?"

DC Jones stood up.

"No guv, It's true, Rice was not a popular fellow. In fact, no one had a good word to say about him. The consensus was that he was nothing short of a bully. All the gossip was of the bitter feud between Rice and Watson. Rice had told Steve Ginn that he had paid someone to graffiti the front of Watson's house as revenge for the attacks on their own properties. Watson had moved out before the attack."

"Well, that pretty much confirms what we suspected. What about Watson's past?" DC Gower stood this time.

"The most interesting fact we pulled up, is that Watson was a top marksman at the gun club, a real hot shot." DC Blackwood interrupted.

"So, if as we suspect, Watson is our man, it's a murder charge. A skilled marksman couldn't accidently shoot a man in the head."

"Anything on CCTV of Watsons movements Grace"

"Not much guv, footage from the neighbouring properties show a black Ford on the street shortly after the shooting. None of them caught the registration number. I'm checking if he used his mobile or bank cards, anytime between eleven and one."

"Thanks team, we need to up our efforts. We don't have enough to obtain a search warrant. I suspect Watson has already disposed of the guns, but you never know, criminals make mistakes, that's how we catch them. Find me something that places Watson anywhere between his and Rice's house, before twelve o'clock on the twelfth of May. This will prove his lying and be enough for a search warrant. Check shops and garages CCTV. On all the possible routes he could have driven to get to the victims address. Team, I need you all to move on this and quickly. Mrs Rice came to the station again this morning. She was close to hysterical. She shouted at me that she knew he did it. We knew he did it. So why the fuck is he still swanning around Scott free? I calmed her down and bought a little time, but if she goes to the press and tells them about Watson, it will seriously prejudice our case. It can't hit the media until we arrest Jack Watson. So come on let's get busy. I want proof within forty-eight hours. The team dispersed, each of them fully aware of the two long shifts that awaited them, unless of course they got a lucky break.

CHAPTER 64

Now that Laura was on the mend, Jack could really focus on the business. First task was to get the paperwork into some kind of order so Laura could make sense of it. To his surprise all the paperwork on his desk was arranged in relevant piles. Invoices owing, invoices to be paid. Delivery tickets and work schedule. He walked out into the workshop to ask who had done this. Jack should have guessed it was young Jeff.

"Well done mate, I owe you one." Jeff looked a little embarrassed.

"While I have got you all here together, I'd like to thank you for all of your efforts since Laura's accident. You have kept the business running, no thriving without me. I will not forget this." All three mumbled their appreciation.

"Now that Laura is recovering well, I am back at the helm. I won't interfere with the way the workshop is being managed. The three of you are on top of it, and whatever the system you are using it is working. When Laura is feeling stronger, I will talk to her about introducing profit share for you all. Stick with me lads and I promise because of what you have done for me you will grow with the company. Now I'm going to get on with my job. Please carry on gentlemen, Thank you once again." He shook Them by the hands and returned to his office.

The order book was still looking healthy, and now Jack had the right mindset to drum up more business. The future was looking bright!

CHAPTER 65

Jack had called Beth earlier in the day, telling her not to cook. As a treat, they could order a Chinese, when he got home, he also asked her to put a few beers into the fridge. As he walked in, Robbie, already in his pyjamas, jumped on him for a cuddle before bed. It was past his bedtime but Beth let him nod off on the sofa. Beth came in from the kitchen with two glasses of cold beer. Her hair was wet and she wore one of Jack's shirts, opened a bit too far for Jack's liking. She noticed Jack look down and quickly with a giggle said sorry and did a couple of buttons up. The white cotton material was straining to hold back her ample bosom. Jack took little Robbie by the hand, and after a quick swig of beer, he said.

"Time for bed my little soldier." Then he took Robbie upstairs. He called back to Beth.

"Choose something from the menu, I know what I want." Robbie was asleep as soon as his little head hit the pillow. Beth was sitting on the sofa sipping her beer, she chose sweet and sour chicken balls. Jack phoned the order through adding his own favourite of chicken Chow Mein and barbeque spareribs. The delivery would take thirty minutes, so Jack finished his beer and went for a shower. It had been a long sweaty day.

Jack was lost in his thoughts, standing under the steady stream of warm water. The sound of the doorbell brought him back to reality. He had been in the shower for over twenty minutes. He put on his comfy jogging bottoms and a baggy t-shirt. When he got downstairs, Beth was already putting the food onto plates, the smell made Jack's stomach rumble. He hadn't eaten since breakfast. Jack poured another couple of glasses of beer and joined Beth at the table. They both were so hungry they hardly said a word during the meal. Only mentioning how good it was. When both plates were empty, Jack told Beth to go into the front room and find a film on Netflix while he cleared up.

"Yes sir." She saluted and gave a cheeky wink. Jack watched her walk away; thinking she was every bit as sexy as Laura.

Jack brought in more beers. Neither of them were big drinkers but they had cause to celebrate. They chatted and laughed often, while half watching a Tom Hanks film. Beth paused the film for a loo and refreshment break. Jack poured two large whiskeys with coke and lots of ice. When Beth sat down next to him, the top button was undone showing a fair amount of cleavage. Jack didn't protest. In fact, he was enjoying the view so much it was distracting him from the film. He had to stop looking as he was getting semi-hard. Beth noticed and laid her head on his lap. Now Jack was getting harder.

"What's this mister? Is that a gun in your pocket, or are you just pleased to see me?" They both laughed. Beth stood up and unbuttoned her shirt.

"This is the third time I have given you an erection Jack, It's about time we did something about it." Jack couldn't take his eyes off her. He was transfixed by her breasts, bigger and firmer than Laura's but the nipples were the same pale pink. She straddled him pushing her breasts close to his face. Jack couldn't resist, he cupped them in his hands and gently teased her nipples which grew remarkably quickly. Beth was gyrating on Jack's manhood. Then she reached a hand behind her and pulled his throbbing penis from his pants. She stroked it slowly, fingers teasing his helmet, she could feel his pre-cum, sticky in her hand. She gasped as Jack took one of her nipples in his mouth and rolled his tongue around it. They were both breathing heavy now. Beth's gripped tightened around his ever-growing cock. She masturbated him with long slow strokes. She raised up and guided him to the entrance of her Virgina which was dripping with excitement. She rubbed him against her lips and slid him inside. Jack thought he was going to explode. Then Laura's face came into Jack's mind and he yelled," Fuck Beth what are we doing?" He pushed her off him and she fell to the floor.

"We must be mad; we can't do this to Laura."

Beth looked a little embarrassed and rejected.

"Come on Jack, you want me as much as I want you. You can't even be near me without getting a hard on." There was venom in her voice.

"I just can't do this to Laura, I love her too much."

"She won't know Jack. I certainly wouldn't tell her."

"We would know Beth. It would destroy Laura. In fact, it would destroy all of us."

"But what about me? Are you just going to leave me in this state?"

"Beth you are a beautiful sexy woman, but I love your sister far too much to risk hurting her." Tears fell from Beth's eyes.

"Fuck you Jack. Thanks for nothing."

"You know I'm right Beth." She ran upstairs and slammed her bedroom door shut. She laid on the bed sobbing. What if he told Laura? She would never forgive her. She thought it would be better if she told Laura first.

Jack just sat there with his head in his hands shaking, repeating the word Fuck over and over. He was already dreading the morning and having to face Beth.

CHAPTER 66

The atmosphere was tense, as Jack expected it to be. Beth was busy being busy, Jack broke the silence.

"Beth, we did the right thing, you know that don't you?"

"What do you mean the right thing Jack?"

"Stopping when we did, before it went too far."

"Your cock was inside me Jack, that constitutes fucking where I come from. So, we did go too far." She spoke with the same venom as the night before.

"I'm sorry Beth, we both had a bit too much to drink and lost control for a few minutes."

"Yeah, yeah Jack blame the booze if it makes it easier for you. That doesn't explain why you get a hard on so easily around me."

"I don't know what to say Beth. We made a mistake. We can't tell Laura; it would destroy her."

"Ok Jack, so it's our dirty little secret. I'll look after Robbie until Laura comes home. We can carry on as if nothing happened." If only that was possible Jack thought. He agonised over his betrayal of the woman he adored more than life itself. The woman who has just given birth to their second little miracle. He felt sick. Should he tell Laura? Would she be able to forgive him? He doubted that. Jack couldn't risk losing his wife. He just hoped to God that Beth didn't tell either. Why would she? She would risk losing her sister, unless of course she lied about what actually happened.

CHAPTER 67

Beth and Robbie were looking out of the front window as Jack parked his car. He opened the door and out came Laura, with Rosie in her arms. Beth felt a twinge of guilt. "Mummy's home Robbie." The little fella banged excitedly on the window.

"Hi Robbie, did you miss me?" Robbie nodded and cuddled Laura's leg.

"You look wonderful Laura." Beth said embracing her sister and kissing the new arrival on the head. Jack felt relieved that Beth was acting as normal. "Thank you so much Beth, for all you have done for Jack and Robbie. You are a star, sister."

"Don't be silly, you would have done the same for me."

"Any chance you can help out for another couple of weeks? Until I get my strength back." Jack held his breath.

"Sorry sis no can do. I have a job to start next week. My stint of being a surrogate mother is over. I'm sure mum will help out. Give her a call."

"Good for you Beth, and thanks again."

"Right, I am going to head off, leave you two love birds to it. I'm sure you have a lot of catching up to do." Beth said with raised eyebrows. Laura laughed, "I'm a bit too tired for any shenanigans." Jack laughed along with the sisters.

"Have a great weekend. Speak soon."

"Cheers Beth, take care," Jack said opening the front door to let her out. Their eyes didn't meet.

Laura called her mum. Gene was only too happy to help out. Telling Laura, she would be there bright and early on Monday. She was surprised to hear about Beth's new job. Moaning that she was always the last to know.

CHAPTER 68

Gene was there early, as promised. Jack let her in, as Laura was still in bed. Gene immediately busied herself with making Robbie some breakfast. Jack was just finishing his toast when a puffy, tired eyed Laura came into the kitchen. He gave them all a kiss and thanked Gene for helping out.

"I have to dash; I have a couple of important meetings to attend first thing. Wish me luck."

"You don't need luck my handsome man, You're the best." Jack could always rely on Laura for support. Laura asked her mum if Beth was excited about starting her new job. Only to be told there was no new job. This left

Laura baffled. Why had her sister lied to her? Why didn't she want to help her with the children? She was only too happy when it was just Jack and Robbie. Laura was never one to let things fester. She phoned Beth.

"Hi Laura, what's up?"

Why did you lie about the job Beth? If you didn't want to help me, all you had to do was say."

"It's not that I didn't want to help."

"Then what is it then?"

"Jack asked me not to say anything."

"Say anything about what? What are you talking about Beth?"

"It's nothing really. The other night we had a few drinks to celebrate the news that you were coming home,"

"I'm listening."

"Well Jack got drunk and made a bit of a pass at me."

"What do you mean, a bit of a pass? What happened?" Laura's voice was now getting angry.

"One minute we were laughing and joking, the next he was kissing me, his hands were everywhere," Laura listened without speaking, her heart was pumping, the anger rising.

"I pushed him off and he apologised. He was embarrassed and said he didn't know what came over him. He pleaded with me not to tell you."

"And is that it, nothing happened? You didn't kiss him back?"

"No Laura, I wouldn't do that to you. He was drunk and got carried away. He loves you Laura."

"Yeah, so much so he tried to get into your knickers." Nothing happened Laura. Don't say anything to Jack, he already feels bad enough. I thought it best if I kept away for a while."

"Bye Beth." Laura cut the line. Beth tried to call her back but she wasn't answered.

Jack got home a little after six. Gene had left a half an hour earlier.

"Hi babe I'm home." There was no response. Laura was sat at the kitchen table, tears rolling down her cheeks.

"Laura, what's wrong? Has something happened?" Beth crossed his mind.

"How could you do that to me Jack?"

"Do what? What are you talking about." He tried to feign confusion but his face was as guilty as sin.

"I'm in hospital in a coma, fighting for my life, giving birth to our child and your trying to screw my sister." Her voice was filled with anger and hurt.

"What did she tell you Laura?"

"Oh, nothing much, only how my drunken husband tried to get into her knickers."

"It wasn't like that Laura."

"Well please enlighten me Jack. what was it like?"

"She came on to me Laura, I don't know what she told you."

"Funny that she said it was the other way around. You, Jack, hands all over her, trying to kiss her."

"No Laura, you have to believe me, it was her that made the move. She sat on my lap and unbuttoned her shirt exposing her breasts. She kissed me. I pushed her off and she was annoyed, rejected."

"So exactly how far did it go Jack?"

"That's it, a drunken fumble, nothing more." Jack preyed the Beth had not told her that he was inside her. The tears had stopped. Jack had never seen his wife look so sad, beaten."

"Who do I believe? My husband or my sister? Or are you both equally to blame? I bet you have had a right laugh behind my back."

"It wasn't like that Laura. You have always been, and always will be the only one for me. I love you so much." Laura knew he meant the words; she couldn't stop the feeling of betrayal.

"I need time Jack; you can stay in the spare room." She left Jack sitting alone with only his thoughts, his guilt for company. He had never felt so low, how could he have done that? Jack always looked to blame others for all the bad things that had happened in his life. Not this time. The blame sat squarely on his shoulders.

He was gutted that Beth, told Laura, even after promising not to. He thought of calling her, but that would only make matters worse. He was grateful that she didn't tell the whole storey. And hoped she never would.

CHAPTER 69

Jack was at his desk in the workshop early the next morning. He didn't wake Laura, just gave her a kiss. The second of his two meetings the previous day, seemed to go very well. It was for a contract north of a million pounds. The client was Travel Lodge. The contract was to supply and fit wardrobes and a desk with a matching chair to four hundred rooms. Jack quoted three thousand five hundred per room. His phone rang, bang on the time agreed. Mr. George head surveyor at Travel lodge was on the line.

"Mr Watson, thank you for your time yesterday. We were very impressed with your presentation and even more impressed with you as an individual."

"Thanks," said Jack feeling he needed to contribute to the so far one-sided conversation.

"The MD would love to have you on board, there is just one stumbling block. The price," Jack had expected to be knocked down a bit, he had added to his quote as a sort of tactical back up.

"Is there any room for movement Mr Watson? Bearing in mind this has the potential to become a rolling contract. When Travel Lodge is not building new hotels, it is often updating the old, tired ones." Jack was very calm and chose his words well.

"How much are we talking per unit Mr George? I have kept my costs and profit margins low."

"Knock off a hundred pounds a unit and we can sign the contract today." Jack had been expecting double that.

"You're a hard man Mr George. We have a deal."

"Great to have you on board Mr Watson. I think we can drop the formalities; you can call me Nick." Jack laughed, "And you can call me Jack. "See you at one."

The contract signing was a formality as all the terms and conditions had been discussed the day before. Jack was so proud he wanted to call Laura with the news but decided against it. She asked for time, so Jack thought it best to wait until she asked about the business.

Back at the workshop, Jack called a meeting to break the news to the lads. They all sat quietly as Jack went through the details of the contract. Michael asked. "Will we be taking on more staff boss?"
"Yes Michael. I am interviewing two wood machinists this week. That will allow you three, to concentrate on hitting the build target. We need to be delivering ten units per week for forty

weeks," Billy gave a whistle. "It seems a lot to take on Jack?"

"We can achieve that lads and still continue with our bespoke furniture items. I have secured a twenty per cent up-front payment for materials. Before our first delivery date I want us to have thirty units made, that way we will always be two weeks ahead, in case of any unforeseen delays. There are heavy penalties for being late. If on the other hand they are not ready for us, they will pay five hundred per week for storage. So, you see it needs to run like a well-oiled machine from both sides."

Billy asked about storage. "Where are we going to keep all the materials and the thirty wardrobes and other items?"

"Good question Billy. I'm ahead of you there. I have rented another unit three doors down. That's where all the materials and finished items can be stored. There is space for two new saw benches which I will order this afternoon."

"Jesus boss, you sure know your onions." Michael interrupted. "I have just one concern."

"Go on Michael, the floor is yours."

"I don't see how we will be able to keep ahead once we have to start fitting out the hotel."

"I'm ahead of you there as well. I have already negotiated a deal with the team I use for installing the kitchens, they will take care of the fit out. Before we start on this project, I suggest a company day out at the horse racing. Any objections?" Heads shook. "I thought not." Jack laughed. "Now all of you pack up what you're doing, I'm taking you to the pub. This is a massive day for us gentleman, let's celebrate."

Jack also realised that Laura would soon be extra busy, there would be thirty-four grand a week going through the company accounts from Travel Lodge alone. Perhaps they would need to hire another accountant. This would need to be Laura's decision.

CHAPTER 70

DI Lock finally got the breakthrough he had been waiting for. In fact, two break throughs. First to announce the good news was DC Jones.

"We discovered from Watsons bank statements that he used his card to pay for a sandwich at a petrol station in Potters Bar. at eleven o'clock on the morning of the twelfth of May." DC Jones walked up to the big screen and inserted a tape. The image on screen showed Jack Watson at the checkout, staring directly at the camera.

"Brilliant work, We were confident that Watson was lying to us, now there is the proof. He left his house well before twelve o' clock on the morning in question." DI Lock couldn't hide the delight in his voice. Next to speak was Grace Williams. "He also used his mobile phone at eleven forty-five the same morning. We got a signal from a phone mast, not two miles from the victims address." DI Lock stood up and congratulated her on her finding. "We have two strong pieces of evidence, proving that Watson is a liar. Why would he lie if he wasn't guilty? We have enough to get a search warrant for both Watson's house and workplace. DS Blackwood, you can sort out the warrant with the magistrate. Let me know when we have it, and I will serve it on Watson personally. Then we can bring him in for a proper chat. I don't think we have enough to charge him yet. Hopefully, we find some more evidence in the searches. Well done all, this has been a great team effort."

CHAPTER 71

Laura had been ignoring Beth's calls and text messages for three days. She needed the time to get her head around the betrayal by her sister and husband. She dialled Beth's number.

"Laura, I have been trying to get hold of you for days. Is everything OK?"

"Well, no, not really. I have been trying to come to terms with the bombshell you dropped on me. I don't get why you felt the need to tell me, if, as you say nothing happened."

"I Had to tell you Laura, I couldn't take the chance of Jack telling you first."

"Jacks version of events differs from yours Beth."

"Oh, I bet it does. I bet he has tried to lay the blame at my door."

"He says you came on to him."

"And you believe him?"

"I have to believe him Beth, if I don't trust in Jack and what he tells me then there is no future for us".

"What about me? I'm your sister for goodness sake."

"Yes Beth. But you have always been a bit too close to Jack, always flirting even in front of me. Jack told me how you walked around the house wearing next to nothing."

"That's rubbish, I bet he didn't mention his constant erections whenever he was close to me?"

"Enough now Beth. I don't want to hear any more on the subject. Time, they say is a great healer, so in time we will put this behind us. Bye Beth, don't call me for a while."

"Take care Laura. I love you sister." Beth said close to tears. Laura ended the call.

Jack arrived home a little later than usual.

"You don't have to avoid me completely Jack. Sit down, I want to talk with you." Jack sat at the dining room table. He braced himself for what was about to happen.

"I spoke to Beth earlier and told her that I believed your side of the story. She didn't like it and accused you of acting like a horny teenager."

"She is something else."

"Enough Jack, she is still my sister. I said I believed you Jack, but your both to blame. I want to put this behind us."

"Laura, I love you."

"I love you too my handsome man. Don't ever give me reason to doubt you again Jack, is that clear?"

"No chance of that. I am the luckiest man alive. I have a beautiful wife, two gorgeous kids, a wonderful home and a successful business." They hugged for a long, long time, both lost in the love that had grown so strong over the years. Laura was amazed at the news about the contract with Travel Lodge. Jack suggested a trip to the seaside at the weekend, just the two of them. Laura agreed and they booked a hotel in Bournemouth.

CHAPTER 72

Eight o'clock on Saturday morning DS Blackwood walked into DI Lock's office proudly waving a search warrant.

"Brilliant, no problem with the magistrates then?"

"none at all guv."

"Nice one. Round up six uniforms. One can search the garage, two downstairs, two upstairs and one the loft. Then you can take a couple over to check on Watson's workshop." Twenty minutes later the team was gathered in the car park. Lock and Blackwood approached.

"Come on then boys, let's go wake up the Watsons. DC Blackwood and I will go in first and issue the warrants. Then

I will call you in. You have all been briefed on your specific search areas?" Nods all round followed by a few random yes sir's.

"Any questions." There were none.

Gene and Ray had arrived early for their baby-sitting duties. It was much easier for them to stay at Jack and Laura's then to pack the kids off to their own house. Jack had packed before bed and the case was sitting by the front door. Laura and gene were washing the last of the breakfast dishes when a sudden loud banging on the front door made them both jump. Gene dropped the plate she was holding and it smashed in pieces on the tiled kitchen floor.

"Open up it's the police." Jack's heart sank. Ray looked at him blankly. "What do they want?" he asked. Jack shrugged his shoulders and went to find out. Jack was greeted by a smiling DI Lock holding some papers in his hand. He could see a number of uniformed police by the gate.

"Good morning, Mr Watson. This is a warrant to search this house and your workplace." He said almost too cheeringly. He certainly loved his job, Jack thought. Jack noticed him glance at the suitcase.

"What the hell do you expect to find?"

"We will let you know when we find it, Now hand over your mobile phone and laptop."

"Am I under arrest?"

"Not yet Jack. Come on lads let's get this over with." Lock gestured to his squad. Inside, Laura, Gene and ray stood together stunned as police seemed to be everywhere, coming from all angles. DS Blackwood asked Jack and his family to sit at the table and he waited with them.

"What the hell is all this about Jack? What have you done?"

"Nothing Laura. They are trying to pin some bloke getting shot with an air rifle on me." Laura's head dropped. "Did you do it Jack?"

"No Laura, They have nothing on me."

"Ray interrupted. "They must have something Jack, they have a search warrant for god's sake."

"So, you're a fucking expert are you Ray."

"Don't talk to my dad like that."

"Sorry." DS Blackwood told them all to calm down. When the search has been completed DI Lock will explain what's going on.

The search's to the ground floor and garage was fruitless. The uniform in the garage thought he had struck lucky, he found a tin of air rifle pellets, which he found contained tiny pins. DI Lock was called up to the loft. He struggled through the hatch; he was not as young as he once was. He wished he had sent Blackwood up.

"Over here sir." Said the uniform, pointing his torch to a box which he found under the roof insulation. DI

Lock bent down for a closer look. Bingo, it was a box of air rifle darts and scattered around were a few air rifle pellets.

"Give me an evidence bag." The young Pc did as instructed. Lock put on gloves and picked up the box by the corners and bagged it.

"You can collect all the pellets and put them into another bag. Good work constable."

"Thank you sir." Lock joined the others at the table.

"We would like to ask you some further questions down at the station Mr Watson." Laura stood up. "Further questions? You mean he has been questioned before?"

"Yes Mrs Watson, I'm surprised he hasn't mentioned it to you. We spoke to your sister as well."

"Jack, what the hell? How much more have you been hiding from me?"

"I didn't want to worry you Laura. I'll be home in a couple of hours. They have nothing on me or I would have been arrested by now." Laura sat back down, Gene holding her crying daughters hand.

"DS Blackwood, you take Mr Watson to the station. I want to ask Mrs Watson a couple of questions. I'll join you shortly." Once the house was clear of all the police officers except Lock, he turned to Laura.

"I'm sorry Mrs Watson, this must be quite a shock for you."

"What do you want to ask me?"

"Does your husband own air rifles?"

"Yes, he has a couple of them."

"When was the last time you saw them?"

"Last year, Jack kept them in the garage. He hasn't used them for years. I was worried that Robbie, that's our son, might pick them up, so I asked Jack to either sell them, or put them up in the loft out of harm's way."

"And what did Jack do?"

"He put them in the loft, I handed them up to him along with tins of pellets."

"Thank you Mrs Watson. I'll see myself out." Laura was now more angry, than upset.

"Did you know the police spoke to Beth." She asked her parents. "No, she never tells us anything." Ray answered trying to give a comforting smile, which looked more like a grimace.

"I can't believe my own sister would keep this from me." Gene spoke. "Jack probably told her not to say anything to you."

That's not all he told her not to tell me about."

"What do you mean?"

"Nothing. Beth is a lying, conniving little bitch." Gene and Ray looked at each other, a look that said it was best not to ask any more questions.

CHAPTER 73

Jack sat in the interview room at Hertfordshire police station. He anxiously tapped his fingers on the table. Alone, waiting to see what the police had discovered. He remained confident that they couldn't prove anything, or as he said to Laura he would be under arrest, not brought in for questioning. The four walls of the room were white painted brick, cold and uninviting. There wasn't a mirror on the wall so he assumed his every move, wasn't being observed. There was a small camera above the door, it's little red light flashing intimidatingly. Jack jumped as the door was pushed open. In walked DI Lock and his trusty sidekick DS Blackmore, carrying a folder under his arm. They sat opposite Jack. Lock began.

"Hello again Jack. For your information we are going to record this interview. You have the right to have a solicitor present if you wish."

"I would like a solicitor present." Jack said smugly raising his right eyebrow.

"Fair enough, do you have a solicitor Jack? Or shall I call the duty solicitor?"

"I'll Have the duty solicitor."

"Ok, your choice, It's only a couple of questions Jack, then you can be on your way. The solicitor could take hours to get here." Jack thought long and hard, he decided it would be in his best interests to have legal representation.

"I want a solicitor." Jack said staring blankly at the bare wall to his left. The two detectives left the room. Shortly after, a young PC came in and stood by the door in silence.

Two hours later, a sweaty little fat fella in a poor fitting tweed suit came rushing in. he was in his fifties, balding and obviously very unfit.

"Mr Watson, I'm Stan Granger, the duty solicitor." He wheezed. Offering Jack his hand, which Jack reluctantly shook as briefly as possible, he could feel the sweat beads on his chubby little hand. He advised Jack that it would be frugal to answer the questions at this stage as no charges had been made.

"If they push too far or step out of line, I will intervene. Otherwise, I will remain quiet. If any question makes you feel uncomfortable and you would rather not answer, that's fine."

Jack sighed, "Ok let's get this show on the road. Granger left the room, returning twenty minutes later, accompanied by Lock and Blackwood. Again, the police sat opposite Jack, Granger sat to his left. The young PC was asked to leave the room. DI Lock opened his file clicked the recorder and began the interview.

"Interview commencing at twelve forty-five, Present are DI Lock, DS

Blackwood, Jack Watson and the duty solicitor Stan Granger." Jack shuffled uneasily in his seat. not knowing what was coming.

"Mr Watson, we would like to ask you a few further questions, to assist us in our inquiry into the murder of Brian Rice. You told us in a previous statement that you left your house after twelve mid-day on the twelfth of May this year, is that correct?"

"That's correct."

"That's a lie Jack," DI Lock pushed a photograph in front of Jack." For the benefit of the tape, I'm showing Mr Watson a photo of himself at the check-out of a petrol station at eleven-thirty on the twelfth of May. How do you explain that Mr Watson?" Jack was rocked by this, but managed not to show it, stay calm he told himself.

"I Must have been mistaken about the date, I'm a busy man."

"You also stated that on the twelfth you had two appointments with clients. Is that correct?"

"yes, if that is what I said."

"We know you used your mobile before mid-day on the twelfth, your signal was picked up by a mast."

"So, what's unusual about me making a phone call? I make them all the time."

"The signal shows you were twenty miles from the address of your first appointment, where were you Jack?"

"I have no idea, why don't you tell me?"

"You were two miles from the house where Brian Rice was shot and killed."

"I can't explain that, just a coincidence." Lock laughed and shook his head.

"You also made a statement to the fact that you had at some point owned two air rifles, is this correct?"

"Yes, that's correct."

"And you told us that you sold them to some bloke down the pub, is this also, correct?

"Yes." Jack huffed, showing obvious signs he was growing tired of this. Again, he told himself to remain calm.

"When did you sell them Jack?"

"Bloody hell, I can't remember."

"Think Jack, it's important, Last week, last month, six months ago, last year, five years. When Jack?"

"Must have been around three years ago, I hadn't been to the range for ages."

"Another lie." Gasped lock. "How old is your son Jack?"

"What has Robbie got to do with this."

"Just answer the question."

"Three and a half."

"Did you sell the gun before or after he was born?" Alarm bells began to ring in Jacks head. Where is this leading? "I'm not sure, maybe after."

"It's interesting Jack, we asked your wife about the rifles, when she last saw them, and she stated, let me check. Lock pulled out his note pad and flicked through the pages. "Ah yes, to quote Mrs Watson. "About a year ago, I asked Jack to either sell them or put them up in the loft." End of quote. So, you had them a year ago?" Jack was now

393

sweating. He looked to his solicitor who sat blank faced.

"She must have got it wrong."

"No Jack she clearly remembers passing them up to you in the loft along with ammunition."

"Remember, my wife has just had a serious illness, a major swelling on the brain. She is obviously confused." Jack was clutching at straws.

"Did you at any time store them in the loft?

"No." DI Lock pulled another photograph from his folder and pushed it towards Jack.

"Do you recognise this jack? For the benefit of the tape, I am showing Mr Watson a photo of a tin of air rifle darts."

"I need to take a break. Jack turned to Granger for help. "My client has requested a break and as he is not under arrest, I think this is a reasonable request." Lock shrugged at Blackwood, "Interview suspended at thirteen-thirty. He gathered his paperwork and left the room with Blackwood.

Jack was given a cup of tea. Granger told him to stay calm. In his opinion, so far, they didn't seem to have much hard evidence. Jack felt as though the noose was tightening.

CHAPTER 74

Interview with Mr Jack Watson resumed at fourteen hundred hours. All present as before.

"Now Jack do you recognised the photograph?"

"It's darts for an air rifle, what about it?"

"Are they yours Jack?"

"I very much doubt it. I told you I got rid of the guns years ago."

"I don't believe you," Jack shrugged his shoulders and didn't respond. "For the benefit of the tape Mr Watson shrugged his shoulders. Is this a product you would have used in the past?"

"Yea I suppose so."

"Can you explain then, how they came to be in your loft at home?" Jack took a big breath. "No comment"

"We found them under your loft insulation."

"No comment."

"Let me tell you what I think Jack. After we questioned you the first time regarding the shooting of Brian Rice. You panicked, didn't you?"

"No comment."

"You got rid of the guns along with the tins of pellets and darts. We know they were up there; we have a statement from your wife. But you missed a tin and we also found a number of loose pellets up there as well. Lock showed Jack a photo of the pellets."

"No comment."

"Jack, why not just admit it, you shot Brian Rice over a feud that went too far?"

"No comment." Granger was now looking uneasy. "My client has answered your questions DI Lock, either charge him or let him go."

"Thank you, Mr Granger. As you are aware we can question your client for up to twenty-four hours without charge." Granger gestured with the palm of his hand. "Pray continue inspector."

"We found a print on the tin which is being analysed as we speak. The darts will be examined by forensics to see if they match the one used to kill Brian Rice." Every time he heard that name, Jack saw Brian's face. "Tell us the truth Jack."

"No comment."

"Interview ended at fourteen twenty-five. OK Watson your free to go. I saw the suitcase in your hall, don't go far Mr Watson." Jack ignored that comment. Lock and Blackwood left the room. Granger advised Jack to get a solicitor and fast.

CHAPTER 75

Jack declined the offer of a lift home from the police station. Even though his house was over three miles away he decided to walk. He needed time to clear his head. It was bad enough getting grief from the police but he was far more worried about facing his wife. She will be furious, distraught. Should he deny any involvement in the shooting? That would mean lying to Laura. If he tells her the truth, would she disown him? Or stand by him. He was about to find out as he walked into his house.

Laura was sat at the dining table on her own.

"Hi Laura, where are the kids?"

"my mum is looking after them for a few hours, I couldn't cope. So, they didn't charge you then?"

"No, I told you, they have nothing on me."

"Jack, I am going to ask you one question. Think carefully before you answer. If you lie to me, we are finished." Jack braced himself, he knew what was coming.

"Did you shoot that man Jack?" He bowed his head and closed his eyes as if in deep thought.

"Yes Laura, I did. I meant to hit him in the shoulder but the gun slipped. It was an accident." Laura fought back the tears.

"You have been lying to me all along, you even got Beth to cover for you."

"I haven't been lying to you Laura. I didn't tell you because I didn't want to worry you."

"I asked you about this when the police came to the house and you just fobbed me off. That's lying in my book Jack.

What else have you lied about? Did you sleep with Beth?" Now the tears were flowing, her voice was a mixture of anger and pain.

"No Laura, I didn't. Please believe me." She shook her head.

"I don't know what to believe anymore. You have ruined everything."

"We will be ok darling. They haven't charged me."

"That's not the point. You can't be stupid enough to believe I can carry on living in the same house as a murderer?" The words stung.

"I'm not a murderer Laura, it was an accident."

"You will have to admit to it Jack. Tell the police what you just told me."

"I can't Laura. They won't believe me."

"It's the only way Jack. You shot a man who is dead. You need to pay for your actions."

"I need to talk to a solicitor first. To see what my options are."

"Your options are that you're going to prison Jack. The question is for how long?"

"Don't say that Laura, it was an accident."

"Grow up Jack. A man is dead because of you and some stupid vendetta. It makes my blood boil to think about all that money we wasted on your counselling."

"What has my counselling got to do with it?" Laura shook her head in disbelief.

"When we met Jack, you were a lost, troubled sole. Months of counselling taught you how not to bottle things up. We decided then that there would be no secrets between us. If anything was troubling either of us, we talked it through, solved it together. Why didn't you come to me Jack?"

"I don't know Laura; I didn't think it was important. I never thought it would eat me up."

"Where are your guns." This question took Jack by surprise.

"I threw them in the river after," Jack paused.

"Did you tell that to the police?"

"No, I told them that I sold them a few years ago."

"Great, I told them we put them in the loft a year ago."

"I know they told me that."

"Bloody hell Jack, they could call me as a witness for the prosecution. They could make me testify against you."

"No, it won't come to that. Calm down."

"Don't tell me to bloody calm down. Because of your stupid ego, I have to bring up Robbie and Rosie without a father. What do I tell them when they ask where's daddy? Do I tell them you're a murderer?"

"Don't keep saying that Laura," Jack's voice was raised. "I am not a murderer; It was an accident."

"What will I do Jack, while your rotting in some prison cell?" Laura was prone to over dramatizing. Jack embraced his crying wife.

"It won't come to that Laura, I didn't want him dead, I will be haunted by this for the rest of my life. If it goes to court, they will believe I didn't mean to kill him."

"It's still manslaughter Jack, however you want to dress it up." Jack kept silent; he knew Laura was right. He needed a good solicitor, and as Granger said, it was a matter of urgency.

CHAPTER 76

Monday morning, Jack left for work as normal. But he knew nothing was going to be normal ever again. He had a couple of clients to visit, to discuss more orders. Then he planned to go to the workshop to check on how the lads were doing, getting ready for the kick off of the big contract he had secured with travel lodge. Jack always enjoyed meeting up with satisfied customers, especially ones who placed new orders, and or recommended him to their friends and families. There is no better form of advertising than word of mouth. Today was different, Jack felt different. He knew he had to put on a brave face and try to keep the business moving forward, But the truth was, Jack was a very worried man, frightened of losing everything he and Laura had worked so hard for. His biggest fear was losing Laura. Jack couldn't contemplate life without her, he would rather be dead.

After his morning meetings, which went very well, Jack couldn't face going to the workshop, he gave Billy a quick call, and told him he had things to do and they could catch up in the morning. Jack needed to be on his own, to consider his options, if, as he feared he ended up in prison.

Jack Pulled into the Bulls head car park. Armed with his laptop and notepad he headed inside. The place was almost deserted, save for a few old codgers at the bar. All sipping their pints and lost in thought. There was also a couple in the back bar, playing pool. Jack put his things on a table in a little alcove out of sight of the other punters. He ordered a large Jack Danials with coke and lots of ice and a pint of lager chaser.

It didn't take him long to decide that his best chance of safeguarding his company, in case of a long sentence, was to promote Billy. Perhaps make him a partner. He called Laura who immediately thought this to be a great idea, she had been thinking along the same lines. Jack called Billy again and arranged a meeting with him for ten o'clock the following morning. The barmaid came over and Jack ordered the same again. His next call was to Nick George at travel lodge. Jack explained the situation with Laura's illness and recuperation and told him he needed to spend time at home, helping with the kids.

"I understand Jack. How does this impact our delivery dates?" Nick's tone was one of concern.

"It won't Nick, I have a projects manager in place to look after the contract from start to finish. I'd like to introduce him to you this week, if your available?"

"Great, I'm free on Thursday afternoon."

"We can meet at the workshop; you can see all the materials on site and inspect the units we have made already."

"You already have samples?" His tone had changed to one of excitement.

"More than samples Nick. We have made all the units for the first two call offs."

"Excellent Jack, That's terrific news. See you on Thursday."

"I look forward to it." Jack ended the call.

Next task, find a solicitor. He spoke to three local firms, the last was his choice. A Mrs Hudd, she was very direct. She told him there was no need for her involvement unless the police either arrested him or brought him in for further questioning. Jack neither denied nor confirmed his guilt to Mrs Hudd.

Jack sat and sipped his third large Jack Daniels. He should have been pleased with his afternoons work, but still felt flat. He glanced at his watch; shit, he couldn't believe he had been sitting there for nearly three hours. He needed the toilet and as he stood up, he felt a bit lightheaded. The pub had filled up significantly. Jack stumbled on the steps down from his alcove seat and knocked into three young lads who looked like construction workers.

"Take it easy you piss head." One of the lads barked at Jack. Rage came over Jack, he spun and threw a punch at the one doing the bad mouthing. The punch was easy to dodge, Jack was clearly drunk. One of the other lads landed a peach of a right hand into Jacks face, causing his nose to bust. He hit the floor clutching his nose, the blood seeping through his fingers. The three lads walked out of the pub, Hurling insults and abuse at Jack. The barmaid helped him up and gave him a handful of tissues to stem the blood.

"Time for you to go sunshine. Shall I call you a taxi?"

"No Thanks, I only live up the road, I can walk."

"If you're sure luvy? Take care."

Jack took a big swig from his glass and gathered his belongings. After a quick visit to the toilet, where he tried to clean himself up, He headed home. Hoping Laura would be resting. He didn't need another roasting from his wife.

CHAPTER 77

Laura surprised Jack when he arrived home bloodied, and four sheets to the wind. Yes, she gave him a telling off for being in that state, but she seemed mildly amused by her drunken husband. On a serious note, she told him to man up and face responsibilities. She also made him promise that he would not be seeking to get revenge on the bloke who punched him. Jack assured her that he had learnt his lesson.

After a shower, and several black coffees Jack and Laura had talked long into the night on how best to prepare for the likelihood that Jack wouldn't be around for a considerable amount of time.

The following morning Jack called his three most trusted employees into the office.

"Sit down gentleman, I need to talk to the three of you."

"What's wrong boss? Are you not happy with our performance?" A worried looking Michael asked.

"Quite the reverse Michael. I couldn't be happier. The company is in a very strong position."

"Then what?" Jeff chipped in.

"I need to restructure the company."

"What do you mean? Why?" It was Billy's turn to show concern.

"I am going to be honest with you. I have got myself into a rather large pickle, which I don't want to discuss at this time. Suffice to say there is a strong chance I won't be around for a while."

"How long is a while?" asked Jeff. Jack just spread his arms and puffed his cheeks.

"You will know when I do." All three were baffled but thought better than to push for more information.

"So, what's the plan boss?" Micael spoke in his cheery Irish brogue.

Jack went over the plan he and Laura had drawn up the previous evening. All three were excited to buy into it, especially Billy who was delighted to be almost stepping into Jack's shoes. His new role, basically put him in charge of the company. Michael's new responsibility was to run the bespoke furniture side of the business, Whilst young Jeff, along with working on the travel lodge contract was given sole responsibility for the craft fairs, which Jack pointed out were an integral part of the business. Michael jumped in again.

"Well boss, that all sounds grand, but what's in it for us?" Jack knew what he meant but decided to tease.

"How do you mean Michael? What's in it for us?" Michael looked at the others for support, none was forthcoming, so he ploughed on, rubbing his thumb and fore finger together.

"You know boss, a pay rise." Jack feigned surprise.

"Oh, I get it, you think because I'm asking you to take on more responsibilities, your entitled to a few extra bob? Is that what you're saying Michael?" Michael now looked a bit embarrassed and wondered why Billy and Jeff said nothing. Billy couldn't hold his laughter back any longer. He blurted out between chuckles.

"He is taking the piss Michael." Michael's head flicked between the laughing Billy and the serious faced Jack.

"Sorry Michael, I couldn't resist. Of course, you all will be getting a pay increase this month, plus Laura is setting up a profit share scheme. The company is called J Watson and family but to show our appreciation for all your efforts, the three of you are to become part of the family business."

Michael punched the air in delight and grabbed Jeff by the arm, spinning him around the floor in what looked like some form of Irish jig.

Jack ended the meeting by saying, "If I'm not around, I'm sure with you three working alongside Laura, the company will be in safe hands.

CHAPTER 78

Jack greeted Nick Green with a warm smile and a handshake.

"Hi Nick, let's go into my office and I'll introduce you to Billy. Would you like a hot drink?

"No thanks, water will be fine." Jack had asked Billy to wear smart clothes for the meeting, to set a good first impression. He wore a Brown blazer over dark chinos set off by a shirt and tie. Jack had to admit he scrubbed up well. After the introductions jack said, "over to you Billy." He thought it would be a good test, show if he was up to this side of the job. Billy took to it like an old hand. First showing off the products already made. Nick was delighted with the quality of the work. Then Billy went on to discuss programming with the aid of programs and charts on the office wall. Nick was impressed. "I love the fact that you will always be three weeks ahead on production, it leaves me in no doubt that you will never be late with delivery. Question, The contract states that if travel lodge are in delay, you will be paid five hundred pounds a week for storage."

"That's right Nick." Billy spoke with confidence.

"You're not going to try and charge us more because you have three times the amount made?" Billy responded without a glance at Jack. "No of course not, it is our choice to make more than required."

"Excellent, I am more than happy with your set up here Jack and will report back to the MD this afternoon. Here's to a long and fruitful partnership." He raised his glass of water in salute. After he left, Jack congratulated Billy on the way he handled the meeting.

Jack was about to phone Laura when the door to his office crashed open causing him to drop his phone. "What the fuck?" Jack looked up to see DI Lock and DS Blackwood, along with three uniformed officers. Lock began.

"Jack Watson I am arresting you on suspicion of the murder of Brian Rice. You do not have to say anything. But it may harm your defence if you do not mention when questioned something you later rely on in court. Anything you say may be given in evidence." Jack remained silent.

"Cuff him."

"There is no need for handcuffs" Jack pleaded, "Let me walk out with you."

"Cuff him and put him in the car." Lock was insistent. Two uniformed officers frogmarched Jack out through the workshop, past Jack's gobsmacked staff.

"Is there anything I can do?" Asked a worried Billy.

"Let Laura know I have been arrested and tell her I will call her later if I can." Jack barely had time to finish his sentence before he was out of the door heading for the waiting police car.

Billy walked into Jacks office to make the call to Laura. It was a call he didn't relish making. He was surprised by how calmly Laura took the news, almost as if she had been expecting Jack to be arrested.

CHAPTER 79

The duty sergeant at Hertford police station, booked Jack in, so to speak. He asked him if he understood the charge against him to which Jack simply nodded. The cuffs were removed and Jack was asked to empty his pockets. He was told to remove his wedding ring and watch. Jack wanted to keep his ring, but the sergeant told him that where he was going, it wouldn't last five minutes. He used his one allowable phone call to inform Mrs Hudd of his incarceration. She told him she would be there in a couple of hours.

Jack was led to a cell and the door was promptly locked without ceremony.

After almost two hours of berating himself for his stupidity and wondering how he was going to get out of this mess, The cell door opened.

"Your solicitor is here Watson, come with me." The young PC who was guarding the door on his last visit to the station said solemnly.

Jack was led into an interview room. Mrs Hudd greeted him with a warm handshake and a smile, "Please sit-down Mr Watson."

"Call me Jack."

"OK Jack and you can call me Sandra." Mrs Hudd was in her late thirties and very attractive in a hard sort of a way. Her hair was pulled back tight to her head, held in place by a gold pin. Circular glasses which sat on her high cheek bones, highlighted her big brown eyes. She had a good figure, tall and slim. Her grey dress suit, and black shoes looked expensive.

"The police have briefed me into the charges against you." Jack was confused. "What do you mean charges?"

"The CPS want you to be tried for murder, and manslaughter. They often do this to safeguard a conviction of some kind." Jack shook his head and shrugged his shoulders still baffled.

"Jack it would be prudent for you to respond to the questions in the upcoming interview with the response, NO COMMENT." This will annoy the detectives but it will show us what evidence they have against you. Then we can discuss our options before giving a statement."

"You're the boss Sandra." Jack saluted. She knocked on the door and asked the young PC to tell DI Lock that Mr Watson was ready to be interviewed.

CHAPTER 80

Not long after, Mrs Hudd returned to the interview room, accompanied by Lock and Blackwood. Blackwood informed Jack that the interview was being recorded and pointed up to the small camera above the door. Lock started. "Interview with Mr Jack Watson. Start time sixteen thirty. Also, present are Mrs Sandra Hudd, the accused's solicitor, DS Blackwood and me DI Lock.

"Jack, you can save us all a hell of a lot of time here by simply telling us the truth." He stared at Jack without blinking. "Did you shoot Brian Rice on May twelfth this year?" The question took Jack by surprise, he looked to

Sandra for guidance. She smiled and nodded for him to continue.

"No comment."

"We know you lied to us about your whereabouts on the day in question."

"No comment"

"We also know you lied about keeping your air rifles in the loft."

"No comment."

"You also lied about selling them to some bloke down the pub."

"No comment."

"The tin of air rifle darts that we found in your loft, are you still saying didn't belong   to   you?"

"No comment."

"We found a fingerprint on the tin Jack." Sandra interrupted, "Are you saying the print belongs to my client Inspector?"

"Unfortunately,   the   print   was inconclusive, too smudged to give a clear reading, although it was a partial match."

"Please continue inspector." Mrs Hudd said aiming a wry smile at Lock.

"The analysts report, shows that the Darts retrieved from your loft are the same as the one pulled from Brian Rice's head." He paused and stared hard at Jack.

"No comment."

"They also match two other darts used on another occasion to shoot Brian Rice in his calf and Steve Ginn In his posterior."

"No comment."

"The Tin of darts we found in your loft held fifty darts, of which forty-seven remained. Three missing. How do your account for that?"

"No comment."

The air rifle pellets, also found in your loft are a perfect match for the ones found at the murder scene of Brian rice."

"No comment." Sandra spoke. "I would like to take a break for a couple of hours to discuss the information you have just delivered, then my client will make a statement." Jack, and indeed the two detectives looked shocked by this revelation.

"Interview suspended at seventeen hundred hours."

CHAPTER 81

Mrs Hudd waited for the light on the camera to go off before she began.

"Jack, the evidence against you is pretty damming. Especially the air rifle evidence. Plus, the fact that you have been caught out consistently lying to the police." Jack sighed, "Are there any positives? What do you suggest I do? Admit to murder? No way."

"Slow down Jack. Tell me about you, start from your earliest memories right up to when you shot Brian Rice."

"I didn't tell you I shot him."

"Don't mess with me Jack, if you want my help start talking."

Jack tried to be as brief as he could, but his story was long and complex. Mrs Hudd sat quietly engrossed throughout. Making several notes along the way. After an hour, Jack's story was told. Mrs Hudd stood up and paced the room, hands on hips, mumbling to herself.

"So, what are you saying Sandra? Have I got any hope?"

My advice is that you plead not guilty of murder. I'm more than confident we can convince any jury that the killing wasn't pre-meditated," Jack winced when she said killing, it seemed all too surreal to him. Like he was outside looking in. "I also suggest you plead guilty to manslaughter on the grounds of diminished responsibilities."

"How does that work?"

"We need to convince the jury, because of what was happing in your life at the time of the shooting, with Laura being in hospital and your history of being abused and wronged that you acted out of character. We need them to believe you had no control over your actions. It's a long shot Jack, but there is a chance, given the right jury."

"What are my chances? Percentage wise."

"Probably seventy-thirty."

"Let me guess, I'm the thirty, right?" Sandra nodded. "You need to make a statement Jack, tell them what happened on the day of the shooting. You need to highlight how angry you were, with what was happening to your wife, how it all got too much for you. This statement could make all the difference Jack. We still have half an hour before Lock will be back, so let's rehearse."

CHAPTER 82

"Interview resumed with Mr Jack Watson at nineteen hundred hours. Those present as before the break. Lock shuffled some papers and continued. "Jack, did you shoot Mr Brian Rice outside his house on the twelfth of May this year?"

"Yes."

"Tell us in your own words what happened."

"The anger had been building up inside me all week. My wife was in a coma, I didn't know if she would live or die. I feared I would lose both my wife and unborn child. I needed to vent my anger on someone or something."

"And you chose Mr Rice. Why?"

"He stole from me some time ago."

"How do you mean stole? Did he mug you?" Jack laughed. "You know full well what happened. He stopped money from my salary when I left STG, Rice was a director there."

"Is this why you shot him before and had his house vandalised?" Before Jack could respond

Mrs Hudd banged the table. "My client was never charged with earlier offences. Please limit your questions to the twelfth of May."

"Apologies, Mrs Hudd," Lock said holding up the palm of his hand as if in surrender. "What happened on that Saturday in May Jack?"

"I drove to his house," blackwood interrupted," Who's house Jack? You need to be specific."

"Brian Rice's house."

"Thank you, carry on."

"I sat in my car and waited for him to come out." Jack Paused, eyes closed as if reliving the moment.

"Carry on."

"I had two air rifles, already loaded. I shot Rice in the shins, I wanted to teach him a lesson," Mrs Hudd gave a little cough as if to say, too much information. "Then my intention was to hit him on the shoulder with a dart from the other rifle," Jack paused, but as nobody spoke, he continued. "Rice was hopping around, shouting out in pain. I finally lined up the shot, but as I pulled the trigger the rifle slipped, forcing the barrel to raise in the air."

"You knew that you had shot Mr Rice in the head, yet you still drove off?"

"I didn't know where the dart hit him."

"But you knew it hit him?"

"Yes." Mrs Hudd gave a slight shake of her head.

"So, Jack you admit, that on the twelfth of May this year you murdered Mr Brian Rice?"

"No, no, No, it was an accident, my only intention was to cause him pain."

"Come on Jack, you're an excellent marksman. You have won several medals and trophies for your sharp shooting. Do you really expect us to believe that you could miss a target by a foot?"

"I told you the gun slipped. I didn't want him dead."

"When did you find out that you had in fact shot Mr Rice in the head?"

"I saw it on the local news, that evening."

"And you didn't hand yourself in?"

"No."

"So, at this point you thought you could get away with the shooting?"

"I don't know what I thought, or what to do. I prayed Rice would recover."

"But he didn't Jack. He died. You killed him," Jack put his face in his hands and remained silent. "If, it was an accident as you claim, why didn't you hand yourself in?"

"I thought no one would believe me."

"And your right Jack no one will." Lock looked at Blackwood with a smile so smug it filled Jack with rage, he launched himself at Lock. He was quickly overpowered by Blackwood and the PC.

"Shall I add assault on a police officer to your charge list Watson?" Lock was now laughing.

"Have you got anything to add, before we type up your statement for you to sign."

"I have told you everything."

"Interview ended at nineteen forty." Mrs Hudd asked if she could have some time with her client so she could explain what happens next. DI Lock agreed, he left the room along with Blackwood.

Mrs Hudd went through the upcoming process with Jack. She explained he would appear before a magistrate court the next day. Where he would be asked to confirm his name, address and date of birth. He would then be held on remand until a Crown court hearing, where he would enter his pleas to the two charges against him. After he would be held on remind until the trial date. In this period the case for the defence would be decided upon. Jack asked, "How long until the trial?"

"Usually around six months."

"Fantastic, banged up for six months."

"Jack, please understand you are on trial for murder, if we can't convince a jury that you were not in control of your actions, you will be banged up for a lot more than six months, that's for sure."

"You said earlier that the murder charge won't stick. If I'm found guilty of manslaughter, what am I looking at?"

"It depends on the judge, how he sees events. Also, on how he views the psychological reports we will present. I would say anywhere between two and twelve years," Jack puffed his cheeks. "We have a strong case Jack, the years of abuse at the hands of your parents, all the times you felt people did you wrong, The loss of your great friend Peter, all these have had a big impact on your mental health Jack, that's what we need to focus on. The fact that you had counselling for years is another strong point for us. It shows your determination to shrug off the demons in your past." Jack was buoyed by Sandra's little pep talk.

"Ok brilliant, it sounds like a plan, where do we start?"

"Whilst you're on remand, I will visit you once a week, and we can build your case."

"Can you phone Laura."

"No problem Jack, once you are on remand, you can call her every day. Do you want her to be at the magistrates court tomorrow?"

"She has enough on her plate. Tell her I will call as soon as I can."

Jack was taken to his cell where he would stay until his court appearance.

Laura sat on her own in the front room of her house, which seemed empty without Jack. Mrs Hudd had updated her earlier and she was grateful for her positivity. Deep down Laura was preparing herself for the worst. Her handsome man was going to prison. She had to be strong for the sake of the children. What was she going to tell them? How do you explain that their daddy won't be around for a long time? She took comfort in the words of her parents, reminding her she was a tough old boot.

Laura flicked the telly on. Bad timing. A female reporter outside Hertford police station.

"Jack Watson, a local man in his thirties has been charged with the murder of Brian Rice, who was shot and killed outside his own home in May this year." The screen cut to a smiling picture of Brian Rice. Then back to the reporter. "Mr Watson will appear before Hatfield magistrates court in the morning." Laura changed the channel. She lost the battle to hold back the tears. All she could keep thinking was, why Jack? Why?

CHAPTER 83

Jack sat in his single cell at The Mount Prison, in Hemel Hempstead. His appearance at Hertford magistrates court was brief. He just confirmed his name and date of birth, The Magistrate remanded him in custody to appear before the Crown court in fourteen days, to enter his pleas. The Old Bailey was to be the venue. Mrs Hudd was jack's first visitor on his second day banged up. She outlined her plan for the defence, it would require a lot of input from Jack. Digging up painful memories from his troubled past. Jack didn't like the sound of this, but Mrs Hudd convinced him that the only chance they had to convince the jury of diminished responsibilities, was to highlight all of the suffering Jack had endured through his childhood and teenage years. Jack told Sandra that he would be more comfortable writing it down than having to talk about it. She had no problem with this but did point out that at some stage, he would have to be interviewed by an independent expert who will advise the court on their findings. Jack was ok with this and said he would have it ready before the plea hearing at Crown Court.

Laura was his next visitor; she really didn't want to come, but she felt that she had to show support for her husband. She knew better than anyone how fragile Jack was. Laura was pleasantly surprised how well her husband looked. He was full of enthusiasm and hope. He went through Mrs Hudd's strategy and Laura agreed it was their one and only chance. They agreed to tell Robbie, Jack had to go away on business. Laura hated lying to the little fella but felt she at no option. Miracles can happen she told herself.

"Stay strong my handsome man. I love you. we can get through this, whatever happens in court." Jack forced out a smile and choking back tears he replied. "Thank you Laura. I couldn't get through this without you. I love you darling."

Mrs Hudd visited every second day. Collecting Jack's memoirs and editing them for maximum affect. She was startled to read about his mother's attack with a Vodka bottle and the constant beatings inflicted on him by his bullying loser father. Although what she read shocked her to the core she was delighted at how strong the case for diminished responsibility was heading. When she read Jack's account surrounding the death of Peter, Mrs Hudd was moved to tears, she felt the pain and anguish in Jack's words. After years of being in and out of care homes and many, many unhappy foster homes, the one man he loved so much he called dad, was taken from him. Poor Jack, she thought to herself, for the amount of suffering, and then the time he had spent in prison, it was incredible how he turned his life around.

Billy also made a couple of visits. The contract with travel lodge was underway and Billy was delighted with the first two instalments. The fitters Jack had arranged finished both weeks one and two, a day early, to the delight of Travel Lodge. It meant their decorators and finishing trades had a day extra to complete. Jack was impressed, he knew his company was in safe hands with Billy and the gang. Once he knew the date for his trial he would discuss any changes required to the business arrangements Jack had put in place.

CHAPTER 84

Jack stood in the dock of court seven at the Old Bailey, in London. Judge Peacock had taken his seat. He looked like most judges, old and uninterested but was as sharp as a needle. Jack looked at the gallery, Sneering back at him was Mrs Rice surrounded by what appeared to be her family and friends. Laura was not present. Jack had been introduced to his barrister, Mr Levitt, before going into the dock. Jack confirmed his name and address. The clerk of the court read out the charges.

"On the count of first-degree murder, how do you plead, guilty or not guilty?"

"Not guilty."

"On the second count of manslaughter, how do you plead, guilty or not guilty?"

"Guilty on the grounds of diminished responsibilities." Mrs Rice stood up and shouted across the court room. "You're a lying bastard, you killed my husband. I hope you rot in hell." This was followed by several here here's from her entourage. Judge Peacock banged his gavel down and demanded order. The court room was immediately quiet. Jack stood calmly, unmoved by her outburst. He refused to look in her direction.

The judge set a date for the trial. Jack was gutted. For the next four months he would have to stew in his prison cell. Mrs Hudd explained, the reason for the wait was due to the complexity of the case. When a plea of diminished responsibility is entered, Both the defence and the prosecution required the time to present their strongest case. She added, "the prosecution will use expert witness opinions to try to discredit your claims Jack We have to present our own experts to endorse them."

That night as Jack lay on his bunk, sleep resisting his tiredness, his mind refusing to shut down. Reality hit him, this would be his home for the next four months, and more likely than not, much longer. He knew he had to find a way to deal with this, but how? Don't crumble Jack, he tried to reassure himself. He knew it was his fault and for the sake of Laura and the children, he needed to man up. Face up to the consequences of his actions. Starting tomorrow when Laura was due to visit. Firstly, decide what to tell Robbie. Then a plan for the future of the business. Jack felt better now that reality had hit home. Sleep came quickly.

CHAPTER 85

For the second time, Laura was impressed by Jack's demeanour. Upbeat and full of energy. Was it just for her benefit? She wasn't sure. They decided it was best to tell Robbie some sort of truth. His daddy was being punished for breaking the rules. Laura knew this would lead to a million and one questions. Three-year-olds always ask, but why? To every statement. Jack had thought long and hard about the business, not just last night but since his arrest. He told Laura he would resign as company director. The best way forward was to open a second company, called, perhaps Watson and family build and design ltd. Laura listened to Jack with great interest. "Make Billy CEO (Chief executive officer) of the existing company. He is to be fully responsible for the travel lodge contract only." Laura nodded." Great idea Jack. Talking about travel lodge, they want us to quote on a new project they are constructing in East London."

"Brilliant, send the drawings and specifications into me. I can prepare the quote."

"Are you allowed to work?" Laura asked looking slightly bemused. "Only while I'm on remand, so we had better make the best of it."

"I see, Ok I will post them this afternoon." Jack smiled and nodded, "Good. Promote Michael to contracts manager for the bespoke furniture side of the business and I think it is only fair to give young Jeff a promotion too. Make him floor manager, in charge of the other joiners and machinists. He can also take on all of the responsibility for the craft fares."

"You really have been busy my handsome man." Laura was surprisingly happy; she was worried that Jack would go into his shell and start feeling sorry for himself. But on the contrary he seemed driven, full of vigour.

"I will leave the salary reviews to you. Obviously, they will all need to be given a pay rise."

"Thank you kind sir, I was wondering where I came in." Laura laughed.

"You're the keystone Laura, without you the business would crumble. We need to be fully focussed on the future. Whatever happens I won't be in here forever."

The warden called time. Laura looked at her watch, surprised how quickly the time had passed, it always did in the company of her handsome man.

"See you next week Jack. Keep your chin up."

Jack waved as Laura headed for the exit.

Back in his cell, Jack tried to convince himself that if he kept busy working on his defence and his business, the following four months would fly by. There is never a good time to go on trial, but three weeks before Christmas had to be the worst. His thoughts turned to Mrs Rice. This would be her first Christmas without her husband. For the first time Jack felt remorse, gut wrenching remorse for what he had done. He saw the hatred in her eyes, both at the hospital and in the court room. He hoped one day she could forgive him. He very much doubted it.

CHAPTER 86

Jack was wrong in his hope that the four months would pass in the blink of an eye. The first two did, taken up by several meetings with Mrs Hudd, building his case. She had warned him on more than one occasion that he would have to sit and listen to the prosecution barrister mocking his guilty plea on the grounds of diminished responsibility. She kept driving home the importance of Jack staying calm. "Show no sign of emotion Jack, the jury will be watching your every move. And most certainly no outbursts. At times you will become frustrated, but the simple fact is that for the most part the prosecution witnesses will be telling the truth. Our defence in contrast will be short and to the point. We will call only a few witnesses. Your councillor, an expert in psychology and perhaps your sister-in-law. My advice to you remains, Don't take the stand Jack." Jack was still undecided as to whether he would testify or not. It would depend on how he thought the case was going.

CHAPTER 87

Jack watched as the jurors were sworn in, one by one, These people, his peers, held Jacks future in their hands. There were six men and six women, an equal split, was this a good thing? Jack thought that perhaps the men were more likely to understand his reasoning for seeking revenge for being stolen from and belittled. Two of the women were young, in their twenties and had already caught Jacks eye. Did one of them smile at him? The other four were of a similar age to Mrs Rice, Jack saw this as a massive negative. The foreman of the jury was one of the four, this Jack thought didn't bode well. He glanced around the court. Mrs Rice sat staring coldly at him, she was with the same crowd who had attended the previous hearing. On the other end of the viewing gallery sat Laura's dad, who gave Jack a warm smile. Laura couldn't attend until after she had given evidence. He still couldn't believe she was called as a witness for the prosecution.

Judge Peacock called the court to order and Jack entered the same pleas as last time. The prosecution was invited to give their opening statement to the jury. Mr Jordon Greaves stood with his thumbs tucked into the lapels of his expensive jacket and approached the jury box. He was in his late fifties and his rosy cheeks and rounded figure gave the appearance of a man who enjoyed life's finer things. "Ladies and gentlemen of the jury. The case for the prosecution will leave you in no doubt to the guilt of Jack Watson," He gestured towards the dock and all twelve jurors looked at Jack. "The evidence is conclusive and we even have the confession of the defendant. You may be asking yourselves why you are here at all? allow me to answer that. The defence have entered a guilty plea on the grounds of diminished responsibilities. The prosecution find this almost comedic and will easily discredit this plea. Thank you your honour." Jack was slightly amused by the performance and he wondered did all barristers watch too much television? Or was it in fact the actors gave brilliant portrayals of barristers at work, Jack surmised it was probably a bit of both.

It was time for the defence to make their statement. Jack's barrister, Ralph Levitt got to his feet and approached the jury. Levitt was a lot taller and leaner than Greaves. He sported a handlebar moustache, which he obviously enjoyed playing with. A tall handsome man, confidence personified. His voice was loud and assertive. "Ladies and gentlemen, Mr Jack Watson is a hard-working family man who has been through much trauma in his life, abused and beaten as a child by his alcoholic mother and bully of a father. In and out of care homes and foster homes. We will show you that the actions of Jack Watson on the twelfth of May were not the actions of a man thinking clearly. His wife was in a coma, Jack didn't know whether she would live or die. Jack Watson was hurting, angry and frustrated. He once again, as in most of his early life felt like the victim. He needed to release the anger that was burning inside of him. He picked Brian Rice, a former colleague who Jack swears stole from him. We will show that Jack Watson was on the verge of a mental breakdown and was not responsible for his actions. Thank you your honour." Judge Peacock called a recess for lunch. The prosecution would call their first witness then. Jack spoke briefly to Mr Levitt and told him that if this was a boxing match he had lost the first round. Levitt shrugged and said. "This is a long fight Jack. We may well lose the first six rounds but then we will come on strong."

CHAPTER 88

First into the witness box was DI Lock. Greaves, "When did you first suspect Jack Watson of the attack on Brian Rice.?"

Lock, "At the scene, Mrs Rice was hysterical and accused Watson of the shooting. She had also accused him of previous attacks of vandalism on her house."

Greaves, "Was Watson questioned about the vandalism?"

Levitt, "Objection your honour, My client is not on trial for vandalism." Mr Levitt sounded a bit annoyed at this line of questioning.

Judge Peacock, "Overruled you may answer the question, but do keep to the events of May twelfth."

Lock, "Yes he was questioned, but he was not charged."

"Greaves, When you questioned Watson about the shooting, did he admit it?"
Lock, "No, he claimed he was at home at the time of the attack."

Greaves, "This was later proved to be one of many lies told by Watson, is that true detective?"

"Lock, "Yes sir, we have CCTV of Jack Watson in a petrol station at the time he claimed to be at home."

Greaves, What else did he lie about?"
Lock, "He lied about how, and when he got rid of his air rifles. He said he had sold them years ago to some bloke in

the pub. In fact, his wife made a statement that she had helped Watson put the rifles in the loft at their new house only a few months earlier."

Greaves, "What happened to the guns?"

Lock, "We later found out that Watson had thrown them in the river."

Greaves, "Would you consider that to be the action of a man who's responsibilities were diminished?"

Levitt, "Objection your honour, supposition."

Judge Peacock, "Sustained, Stick to the questions Mr Greaves."

Greaves, "Yes your honour, What did you find when you obtained a warrant to search Watson's house?"

Lock, "A tin of air rifle darts and some loose air rifle pellets were found in his loft."

Greaves, "How many darts were in the tin?"
Lock, "forty-seven out of fifty."

Greaves, "So three were missing, were these ever discovered?"

Lock, "Yes one was removed from Mr Rice's head," An audible groan came from Mrs Rice,"

Greaves, "And the other two?"

Lock, "They were recovered from an earlier incident in which Mr Rice and his colleague Mr Ginn were shot."
Greaves, "Was Watson questioned about the earlier incident?"

Levitt, "Objection, Irrelevant. My client was never charged with the earlier attack."

Judge Peacock, "Overruled, Be careful Mr Greaves the ice on which you are skating is dangerously thin."

Greaves, "Yes your honour. You can answer the question detective."

Lock, "He was questioned but had an alibi for the time of the attack."

Greaves, "When you arrested Watson did he confess straight away?"

"Lock, "No, he answered all the questions with the same response. No comment."

Greaves, "But then he decided to confess?"

Lock, "Yes on the advice of his solicitor."

Greaves, "Thank you detective, no further questions."

Judge Peacock, "Your witness Mr Levitt."

Levitt, "No questions your honour."

Judge Peacock, "You may step down detective."

Next into the dock was Steve Ginn.

Greaves," How do you know the defendant?"

Ginn, "I gave him a job as contracts manager at STG where I am a director."

Greaves, "How would you say you got along with Watson?"

Ginn, "Very well, he was very good at his job."

Greaves, "Did the defendant get along with everybody in the workplace?"

Ginn, "Mostly yes, he and Brian Rice didn't like each other, this was clear from their first meeting."

Greaves, "the defendant claims that yourself and Brian Rice were responsible for him not being paid the correct salary due, when he left STG. Is this true?"

Ginn, "No, Watson was paid what Brian considered to be the right amount. He logged Watson's hours during his notice period."

Greaves, "Did anything odd happen to you after the defendant left the company?"

Ginn, "Yes I was shot in the bum by an air rifle dart," muffled laughter came from the public gallery. "And my house was spray painted with the word thief on two occasions."

Greaves, "Who do you think was responsible for these attacks?"

"Levitt, "Objection, supposition your honour."

Judge Peacock, "Sustained, I have warned you councillor."

Greaves, "No further questions your honour." Levitt got to his feet and approached the witness box.

Levitt, "Have you had any contact with the defendant since he left STG?"

Ginn, "Yes, we are members of the same golf club."

Levitt, "Is it true that you offered to pay the defendant over two and a half thousand pounds, the shortfall in his salary?"

Ginn, "Yes I did."

Levitt, "What did the defendant say to your offer?"

Ginn, "He would only except half as he wanted Brian Rice to pay the other half."

Levitt, "Did you warn the defendant that Brian Rice was planning to vandalise his house?"

Ginn, "I did."

Levitt, "no further questions your honour."

Greaves stood. "Just a couple more questions your honour. Mr Ginn. Why did you offer to pay the defendant two thousand pounds, if as you testified you thought his salary was correct?"

Ginn, "I wanted to put an end to the attacks and vandalism."

Greaves, "After you paid the defendant the half he asked for, did you or your property suffer from any further attacks?"

Ginn, "No."

Greaves, "No further questions your honour."

Judge Peacock called an end to the proceedings for the day, He warned the jury not to discuss the case with anyone.

CHAPTER 89

Court resumed at ten o' clock the next morning. First to take the witness stand was Laura. Jack felt sick watching his wife stuttering through her oath. Greaves, smiling insincerely began.

 "Mrs Watson, I believe at the time of the shooting of Brian Rice you were in hospital, is that correct?"

Laura, "Yes that is correct." As hard as she tried not to look at her handsome man, she couldn't help herself, as always she was drawn to him like a magnet. She felt as though her heart was breaking. Jack looked lost and alone, she could tell by the bags under his eyes that he hadn't slept well for a long, long time.

Greaves, "What was the reason for your stay in hospital?"

Laura, "I was in an induced coma due to a swelling on the brain."

Greaves, "I am sorry to hear that, I trust all is well now." Laura nodded. "So, you were oblivious to the shooting of Brian Rice?"

Laura, "Yes."

Greaves, "Were you aware of any conflict between your husband and Brian Rice?"

Laura, "I knew he had disputed his pay with STG, but Jack said it was nothing to worry about."

Greaves, "When did the defendant tell you about the feud?"

Laura, "After I got a visit from the police about graffiti attacks on two of STG's directors houses."

Greaves, "Did your husband often hide things from you?"

Laura, "No."

Greaves, "but he did on this occasion?"

Laura, "yes."

Greaves, "The defendant didn't tell you about the shooting until after another visit from the police. Is that correct?"

Laura, "Yes, he said he was trying to protect me."

Greaves, "Indeed. What happened to the air rifles you help store in the loft?"

Laura, "Jack told me he had thrown them in the river."

Greaves, "Before your accident, how was Jack's behaviour?"

Laura, "He was a little quiet during his time at STG. I knew he didn't enjoy working there. He seemed much happier when he returned to his previous employer."

Greaves, "He didn't tell you about the shortfall in his salary either? It seems to me Jack had secrets."

Levitt, "Objection your honour, opinion.

Judge Peacock, "Sustained. We are not interested how it seems to you councillor."

Greaves, "Sorry your honour, no further questions. Mr Levitt had no questions so Laura was excused from the witness box. Jack was shocked to hear the name of the next witness.

Beth avoided eye contact with Jack as she took the oath. Jack's heart was fluttering uncontrollably. Laura had taken a seat in the public gallery next to her dad.

Greaves, "Elizabeth, tell the court your relationship to the defendant."

Beth, "Jack is my brother-in-law."

Greaves, "When your sister was in a coma, you were a great help to the defendant were you not?"

Beth, "I looked after their son, my nephew little Robbie to allow Jack to focus on running his business."

Greaves, "You stayed at the defendants house is that correct?"

Beth, "Yes during the week."

Greaves, "separate rooms.?"

Levitt, "Objection, irrelevant."

Judge Peacock, "Sustained. Don't push it Mr Greaves, the patience of a saint is not something I have been blessed with."

Greaves, "You say you only stayed during the week; How did it occur that you were there on the twelfth of May, which was a Saturday?"

Beth, "Jack told me he had some important clients to visit and asked me to come over."

Greaves, "And you had no idea he was planning to visit Brian Rice?"

Beth, "No, I had never heard of him at that time."

Greaves, "You were also there when the police questioned the defendant about the shooting."

471

Beth, "Yes, I was asked to leave the room."

Greaves, "Detective Lock asked you what time Jack had left the house on the twelfth of May, what did you tell them?"

Beth, "I told them it was after twelve."

Greaves, "And you remember that clearly, how?"

Beth, "It's what time Jack told me he left."

Greaves, "Oh I see, Jack told you he left after twelve, when did he tell you this?"

Beth, "A couple of weeks earlier."

Greaves, "Did you tell your sister about this visit from the police?"

Beth, "No, Jack made me promise not to. He said they had nothing on him and it would all blow over before Laura came home."

Greaves, "Did he ask you to secrete anything else from your sister?"

Beth, "I don't understand."

Greaves, his voice getting louder and more pompous. "Did anything else happen that the defendant asked you to keep from your sister?" Beth looked shocked, she glanced at Jack, his eyes were closed, his hand on his head. She looked behind her, Laura was like a rabbit caught in the headlights. She turned back to face Greaves. "Can you answer the question please Elizabeth?"

Beth, "Yes." Gasps came from many parts of the courtroom. Judge Peacock called for order.

Greaves, "Tell us what else the defendant asked you to conceal from his wife?" How did they know about this? Jack must have told them, was all she could surmise.

Beth, "Jack made a pass at me." Another gasp rang out, Peacock tapped his gavel twice but said nothing.

Greaves, "How do you mean, he made a pass at you?"

Beth, "Laura had been woken from her coma, we celebrated a little too much. Jack was drunk, he tried to kiss me," Laura walked out of the courtroom without looking at either Jack or Beth. "His hands were all over me."

Greaves, "So he molested you?"

Beth, "No that's not what I mean. I pushed him off and he came to his senses."

Greaves, "Thank you Elizabeth." Judge Peacock adjourned for lunch.

During the break Levitt sat with Jack. "They are destroying you out there Jack, Hitting on your own sister while your wife was in a hospital bed."

"That's not how it happened."

"You better tell me the whole story to see if I can salvage anything from this wreckage."

CHAPTER 90

Beth was already sitting in the witness box as the jury returned from their lunch break. After releasing a couple of dry coughs, purely for affect. Levitt began his cross examination. Laura hadn't returned, their dad, Ray, sat glum faced.

"Elizabeth, allow me to applaud your actions while your sister was in hospital. You really stepped up to the plate."

Beth, "It's what any sister would have done."

Levitt, "You were paid for your efforts, is that the case?"

Beth, "Yes, Jack insisted. I would have done it for nothing."

Levitt, "So it was a professional arrangement?"

Beth, "You could say that."

Levitt, "Would you say you are very fond of your brother-in-law?"

Beth, "We are a close family."

Levitt, "Really. Is it not the case that you were jealous of the life, and the man your sister had? You said as much to Jack on their wedding day."

Beth, "No, I was trying to help."

Levitt, "You saw this as an opportunity to step into your sisters shoes, if Laura had not come through, you saw yourself as a ready-made replacement, isn't that the truth Elizabeth?"

Beth, "that's rubbish, how can you say something so horrible?"

Levitt, "You are the one who made a pass at Jack, you wanted him." Beth was now in tears.

Beth, "No."

Levitt, "He pushed you away, you felt hurt, embarrassed, rejected. That's what happened."

Beth, "No that's not true."

Levitt, Did you tell your sister about the visit from the police?"

Beth, "No."

Levitt, "Why not?"

Beth, "Jack asked me not to."

Levitt, But you told her about the amorous encounter even though Jack asked you not to?"

Beth, "I was worried that Jack would tell Laura, so I decided to tell her first."

Levitt, "Did you hope she would throw him out and you could have him for yourself?"

Beth, "No."

Levitt, How are relations between you and your sister now?"

Beth, "We haven't spoken since."

Levitt, "So it's safe to say that Laura believed her husband's version of events and blames you for what happened?"

Beth, "She blamed the both of us. She loves Jack more than she loves me. That is the difference."

Levitt, "No further questions." Jack felt sorry for Beth, she had been made to look bad. He was pleased, in a way because at last he felt that Levitt had entered the fight.

Judge Peacock adjourned for the day, after again warning the jury not to discuss the case.

CHAPTER 91

The morning session on the third day of the trial, was taken up by the opinions of a leading psychologist, Sir Raymond Blake. He left the jury in no doubt that in his considered opinion, the actions of Jack Watson were those of a man entirely responsible for his actions. He went as far as to say that Watson was clearly very bright, cold and calculating. Despite a few futile questions put forward by Mr Levitt, Blakes testimony could only be looked upon as damning. Laura was back in court sitting beside her dad. She tried to smile at Jack, he could see the hope draining from her face.

After lunch, the prosecution called their final witness. Mrs Rice was sworn in. Greaves began, his voice was calm and sympathetic.

"Mrs Rice, I understand this is painful for you, but can you tell us what happened on May twelfth this year?"

Mrs Rice, "That bastard shot my husband in the head." She pointed and sneered at Watson.

Greaves, "Please tell the jury what happened."

Mrs Rice, "Brian opened the passenger car door to let me in, we were heading to the local pub for a spot of lunch. I heard a popping sound and Brian let out a roar of pain. He clutched his lower leg. Then I heard the sound again. Brian's roar, turned to a scream as he now clutched both legs,"

Greaves, "Take your time, would you like some water?" He could see she was starting to get upset. She declined the water and continued.

"I was confused and in a state of panic, our neighbours had come out to see what all the noise was about. Then a different sound, a sort of whistling. Brian went quiet, he fell to the ground and that's when I saw the blood. A red feather was sticking out of Brians temple." She was sobbing now. "After that everything is a blur." Jack looked at the jury, three of the women held tissues and were wiping tears from their eyes. Jack thought he was fucked.

Greaves, "Why did you tell the police that you thought Jack Watson was responsible for the attack?"

Mrs Rice, "That bastard had it in for my husband, first the graffiti on our house, Brian was convinced that both instances had been instigated by Watson. So much so he got someone to return the favour on Watson's house."

Greaves, "Did you ever meet the defendant?"

Mrs Rice, "Yes, he came to our local pub one Saturday lunchtime. Brian, some close friends and I were waiting for our lunch. He came in and started shouting, calling Brian all sorts of names. Credit to my husband, he stayed calm and tried to ignore the insults. Watson caused so much of a fuss he was thrown out."

Greaves, "Did your husband say anything to the defendant?"

Mrs Rice, "He told him to sling his hook, called him a real tough guy, spray painting houses in the dead of night."

Greaves, "Did the defendant threaten your husband?"

Mrs Rice, "Yes he wanted Brian to go outside, shouting I'll show you how tough I am."

Greaves, "Did you see the defendant on any other occasion?"

Mrs Rice, "Yes in the foyer of the hospital he was going out as I was going in."

Greaves, "Did you speak to the defendant?"

Mrs Rice, "Oh yes, I gave him both barrels so to speak. I asked if he had come to finish the job. Brian was in intensive care. He never came home." More tears flowed from Mrs Rice and the three jurors.

Greaves, "How did the defendant react?"

Mrs Rice, "He smirked at me and told the people around us that I was a nut job, and he claimed he had never seen me before. He is nothing more than a lying murder."

Greaves, "Thank you Mrs Rice. No further questions. Levitt stood and approached her with some purpose. "You testified that the defendant came to a pub and hurled abuse at your husband. Please tell the jury what prompted this visit?"

Mrs Rice, "I don't understand the question, sir."

Levitt, "Well it's quite simple! What reason did Jack Watson have to come and see your husband."

Mrs Rice, "I don't know what you mean."

Levitt, "So you expect the court to believe that you had no knowledge your husband sent two thugs to the defendants workshop, damaging property and terrorising an apprentice?"

Mrs rice sat opened mouthed, not quite knowing what to say.

Levitt, "I remind you; you are under oath."

Mrs Rice, "He may have mentioned something about warning Watson off."

Levitt, "He may have mentioned or did?"

Greaves, "Objection your honour, he is bullying the witness."

Judge Peacock, "Overruled, answer the question."

Mrs Rice, "Yes he told me."

Levitt, "So it's safe to say, your husband and the defendant had an ongoing tit for tat feud?"

Mrs Rice, "Yes."

Levitt, "No further questions your honour."

Judge Peacock, "You may step down Mrs Rice.
I think this is a good time to conclude for the day. We will hear the case for the defence tomorrow.

CHAPTER 92

Mr Levitt was in court early that morning. He needed to convince Jack once and for all not to testify. After a brief but heated exchange in which Levitt told Jack in no uncertain terms that the prosecution would tear him apart. Reluctantly Jack agreed. The defence's whole case was aimed at getting the sympathy vote from the jury. What couldn't be doubted was Jack's troubled past.

Judge Peacock invited Mr Levitt to begin the case for the defence. First to be sworn in was retired social worker, Mrs Mary Thorn.

Levitt, "Mrs Thorn would you please tell the members of the jury how you know the defendant Jack Watson?"

Mary, "I was first alerted to suspected abuse by the school which Jack was attending, he was frequently seen to have bruises. Jack would have been eleven or twelve at the time."

Levitt, "What action was taken by social services?"

Mary, "We visited Jack's home. His parents of course denied any knowledge of where the bruises had come from. They said their son was a clumsy sod, always bumping into things."

Levitt, "Jack was eventually taken into care, how did that come about?"

Mary, "We received a call from the hospital to say that Jack had a bad cut on his head. His mother claimed it was an accident but when the doctor questioned Jack, he broke down and told of the years of abuse he had suffered at the hands of his father. He said his mother didn't care about him. He pleaded not to be sent home."

Levitt, "How was Jack, when he was in the care home?"

Mary, "He was very introverted, hardly spoke, he didn't interact with any of the other kids."
Levitt, "What happened then?"

Mary, "Jack was in and out of foster homes for years, he couldn't settle. Most of the families couldn't cope with his mood swings and tantrums."

Levitt, "When did things improve in the life of young Jack?"

Mary, "Jack was placed with foster parents in Tottenham, whose own children had flown the nest. For some unknown reason Jack settled in almost immediately. I was so happy to see him smile for the first time."

CHAPTER 93

Joanne Simms was next to take the stand.

Levitt, "Mrs Simms can you please tell the court your relationship with the defendant Jack Watson?"

Jo, "I was his foster mother."

Levitt, "How was Jack when he arrived in your care?"

Jo, He was a little quiet to begin with, but he hit it off with my husband Peter from the first day. He loved the fact that Peter called him son. They became inseparable. Going to football matches and Jack helped my husband make furniture in his workshop."

Levitt, "Would you say Jack was happy with you and your husband?"

Jo, "He couldn't have been happier, His school work improved out of all recognition. He passed his exams with top grades. We wanted Jack to go to university but he wanted to do an apprenticeship and work alongside Peter."

Levitt, "So all was going well until tragedy struck. Can you tell the court what happened?"

Jo, "My husband had a brain tumour. Jack found him collapsed by his work bench, He died two weeks later."

Levitt, "That must have been an upsetting time for the whole family, How did Jack cope?"

Jo, "He didn't, the change in him was terrible. He went into his shell, hardly spoke to me. He had arguments with one of his stepbrothers. Jack was hurting like all of us."

Levitt, "When did you last see Jack?"

Jo, "After the funeral at the wake which I held at my home. Jack walked up to me, thanked me for all myself and Peter had done for him, he said he would be eternally grateful. He just walked out the door. Today is the first time I have seen Jack since that dreadful day."

Levitt, "Thank you. No further questions. The prosecution had no questions. Judge Peacock adjourned for lunch.

The third witness for the defence was Rose Williams. She told the jury how she had counselled Jack over a period of six months. He visited her once a week for the duration. She explained how in that time he had learnt to leave his demons in the past. He also learnt the importance of talking about issues with his wife. After she had finished her outline of Jack's treatment Levitt asked, "In your opinion was Jack now cured from the effects of his past?"

Rose, "I don't believe that people are ever truly cured, Jack certainly was more confident, he could express his feelings and his concerns. This he was previously unable to do. He could now forgive his mum, and except she had an illness. He came to terms with the death of Peter by remembering the good times he had spent with his foster dad. He wanted to make Peter proud."

Levitt, "So that was it. Until recently you had no further contact with the defendant after your final session?"

Rose, "No, I told him that if at any time he needed to talk, just pick up the phone. He never called."

Levitt, "You have visited him in prison?"

Rose, "Yes, four times."

Levitt, "And how would you describe Jack's mental condition now?"

Rose, "Considering recent events I would have to say he is doing well. He deeply regrets what has happened. He wishes he hadn't let, what he calls the theft of his wages bother him for so long. After all he had gleaned through our sessions, somehow he fell back into his old ways. Perhaps, I like so many others have let Jack Watson down."

Levitt, "Thank you Miss Williams." Again, the prosecution had no questions.

Judge Peacock adjourned for the day as all the witnesses had testified. Tomorrow the summing up would begin.

Jack spoke with Levitt and both were of the opinion that the jury wasn't as affected by the defence as it was by the case for the prosecution. Jack was a worried man. Could they find him guilty of murder? Only time would tell. He told Levitt that his summing up needed to be powerful, if he was to have any hope of swaying the jury.

CHAPTER 94

Mr Greaves approached the jurors and began his closing arguments; He wore a new sky-blue suit for the occasion.

"First I would like to apologise to each and every member of the jury for having to sit through all of the evidence in a cut and dried case such as this. If Jack Watson had an ounce of decency, he would have pleaded guilty of murder and we could of all gone home on day one.

Jack Watson lied to the police on countless occasions trying to cover his tracks. Only when the evidence became so damning did he concoct this cock and bull story about diminished responsibility. We only have to look at his actions after the shooting to see he was of sound mind. He got rid of the guns, he made up an alibi, even tried to coerce his sister-in-law into verifying this lie. Ask yourselves, are these the actions of a man suffering from diminished responsibility or those of a cold calculating criminal? He would have you believe that he only wanted to hurt Mr Brian Rice, teach him a lesson. Claims that the gun slipped causing the dart to hit the victim in the head. Rubbish, we know Jack Watson is an excellent marksman. He meant to shoot Brian in the head. The shots to the legs were just another plan to back up his claims of only trying to hurt Brian if he was caught. Jack Watson knew only too well, a shot to the temple from a high-powered air rifle, could end in the death of Brian Rice. He set out that morning full of hate, and he murdered Brian Rice. After the shooting we are led to believe that the defendant was suffering from diminished responsibilities. Then how did he manage to carry on running his successful business, even winning a massive new contract. No, Jack Watson was functioning fine. He thought he could get away with murder. Ladies and gentlemen of the jury. You have heard all the prosecution witness testimonies, each one like another nail in the defendants coffin. What was the case for the defence, Oh yes poor old Jack had a troubled upbringing. Even so it doesn't give him the right to kill. Based on all the evidence you can only return one verdict and that is guilty of murder.

He returned to his seat. Judge Peacock adjourned for lunch. Mr Levitt knew that he had a mountain to climb if he was to save his client from life in prison.

CHAPTER 95

Neither Jack, nor Levitt enjoyed their lunch. Jack had a quick chat with Laura, who tried her best to convince him that all was not lost. She didn't believe her own words. It all seemed so hopeless. Levitt began." Ladies and gentlemen of the jury, the prosecution would have you believe that Jack Watson is a cold bloodied killer, some kind of a monster. This couldn't be further from the truth. From a young age, any happiness was short lived for Jack Watson. He was and still believes, he is a victim. It seems to Jack that everything he had was taken from him. His parents took his childhood. The powers at be, took Peter away, a man Jack loved as a father. But with help from a great deal of counselling he turned his life around. He married Laura, the love of his life and they set up home and started a family. Then Jack made the biggest mistake of his adult life, he joined a company called STG. He saw this as a career move, an advancement. At first all was ok, until he met Brian Rice, construction director. Brian took an instant dislike to Jack and didn't hide his feelings. Over the coming months he had one intention, get rid of Jack Watson. Perhaps he was threatened by Jack's knowledge, and how good he was at his job. Finally, Brian Rice got what he wanted; Jack resigned. After working his notice period, Jack's pay was two and a half thousand pounds short. Jack accused STG of stealing his money. He was just laughed at. He tried the legal route, applied to have his case heard at an employment tribunal. He got no help from anywhere. STG had a solicitor. Jack had no chance of winning. Another mistake Jack made, was not telling Laura about the money issue, indeed he never told her that he had any problems at work. I think we can safely assume that STG did steal Jack's money. Why else would Steve Ginn offer to pay out of his own pocket? When Laura was laying pregnant in a coma, Jack felt she too was going to be taken from him. The rage in him grew daily. He wasn't going to accept being the victim again. He needed to vent his anger, but on who? The only man he had a vendetta against was Brian Rice, the man behind the theft of his money. Jack lost the plot, yes he wanted to hurt Brian Rice. Kill him no. If he had wanted to kill him why would he bother shooting him in the shins? Obviously, his intension was to cause maximum pain to a man he despised, a man who despised him.

Jack is sorry for what he did. He told me he would carry the guilt with him for the rest of his life.

Ladies and gentlemen of the jury. Jack Watson was not of sound mind on Saturday the twelfth of May. A culmination of all his suffering had broken him. You must find him guilty of involuntary manslaughter, on the grounds of diminished responsibility."

Jack wondered if Levitt's impassioned performance would be strong enough to sway the jury, he doubted it.

Judge Peacock thanked both the prosecution and defence for their closing statements. He told the jury that he would give guidance in the morning before they retired to consider their verdicts. Court was adjourned for the day.

CHAPTER 96

Judge Peacock began summing up.
"Ladies and gentlemen of the jury. I don't agree with the prosecutions opinion that your time was wasted listening to all the evidence and testimony. How else could you make an informed decision. The defendant has pleaded guilty of involuntary manslaughter on the grounds of diminished responsibilities. This is one of three possible outcomes the jury must decide upon.

If you agree that Jack Watson set out on the twelfth of May with the sole intention of killing Mr Brian Rice, you must return a verdict of guilty to the charge of murder. If, however you decide Watson's aim was to inflict severe pain on The victim. These actions, we know resulted in the death of Mr Rice. And you consider his actions on the day, and subsequent days to have been well planned, you have no choice but to find the defendant guilty of manslaughter.

Use the evidence and testimonies to guide you to the correct verdict, one on which you all agree. To clarify.

If you decide Jack Watson's intention was to kill Brian Rice. You must find the defendant guilty of murder.

If you decide Jack Watson wanted to harm Brian Rice and was of sound mind when his actions resulted in the death of Brian Rice. You must find the defendant guilty of manslaughter.

And finally, if you believe as the defence claim, Jack Watson was not of sound mind when he shot Brian Rice.

You must uphold the defendants plea, guilty of involuntary manslaughter."

The clerk of the court ushered the twelve to the jury room. Jack asked Levitt what he thought the verdict would be, based on his extensive experience. He was non-committal. Jack saw this as a glimmer of hope. A tiny glimmer.

CHAPTER 97

It took the jury three days to reach their verdict. Three days in which Jack Watson had a vast mixture of emotions. He knew a prison sentence awaited, but for how long? Would he be an old man when he got out? He allowed himself to dream. The judge could be compassionate and go lightly on the sentence. Was it too much to hope for a suspended sentence?

Judge Peacock, "Will the defendant please rise." Jack stood and took a deep breath as he looked, first at Laura, her parents sitting either side, each holding a hand. At the opposite end of the gallery sat the Rice contingent, their sneering stares hadn't abated. Then he turned to face the judge. "Would the foreman of the jury please stand." She rose slowly to her feet, a piece of paper in her hand. The clerk of the court handed the piece of paper to judge Peacock, after a quick glance, he nodded towards the clerk to continue. "On the charge of murder, how do you find the defendant. Guilty or not guilty?" Jack felt like he couldn't breathe.

"Not guilty." Mrs Rice was up on her feet, yelling, "That's ridiculous, he is a murderer, are you blind as well as stupid?" Judge Peacock banged his gavel furiously. "I won't accept outburst in my court, anymore and I will have you in contempt." She sat back down shaking her head. Peacock, again nodded to the clerk to continue. To the charge of manslaughter on the grounds of diminished responsibility, do you find the defendant guilty or not guilty?"

"Guilty"

"Is that the verdict of you all?"

"Yes." Jack looked up to the heavens, then closed his eyes, trying to keep his breath even. Laura sat head in hands quietly sobbing. There were mumbles from the public gallery. Judge Peacock called for order and addressed Jack.

"You have been found guilty of manslaughter on the grounds of diminished responsibility, You will attend court three weeks from today for sentencing. Be warned it will be a custodial sentence. Take him down. Two officers led Jack away, not before Mrs Rice's voice again echoed around the courtroom. "I hope you rot in jail you bastard. Why did you kill my Brian?"

Jack turned his head and mouthed the words, "They stole from me."

CHAPTER 98

Jack sat, in the courtroom, waiting for the arrival of judge Peacock. He looked at the public gallery. The same faces from three weeks earlier stared back at him. He had only seen Laura once since the verdict, he thought she looked tired. The ordeal he has put her through had clearly taken its toll. The only empty seats were those of the jurors, there was no need for them to be present, they had done their job. The clerk told the court to rise and in walked the judge. Everybody sat except Jack. He looked calm but inside the feeling in his stomach was nauseating. He felt the need to go to the toilet, a similar feeling from the one he used to get before sitting his exams, only worse.

"Jack Watson, you stand before me today for sentencing for the manslaughter of Brian Rice. I have read through the reports and gone over the evidence. I agree with the verdict of the jury. Yes you didn't mean to kill Brian Rice but due to your actions that day you did kill him and should be punished accordingly. I don't believe for a minute that you were unaware of your actions, it was a well-planned attack which ended in tragedy. You will go to prison for fourteen years. Take him down." Mrs Rice smiled at him and mockingly waved and said, "Ta ta." Jack and Laura held a long loving gaze across the court, neither able to smile. "Take care my handsome man, I love you." Jack was gone, taken to the holding cell until his lift to his new home was ready. Levitt came to say his goodbyes. "I know this is tough to take Jack, but it could have been far worse."

"Worse how? How could this be any worse, tell me?"

"Wake up Jack, you could have been sent to prison for life." The reality of the words resonated in Jack's face. "Plus, the best news is the judge didn't set a minimum sentence. If you keep your nose clean you will be out in seven years." Somehow this brought Jack some comfort, facing up to seven years instead of fourteen was much easier. He could be out well before his fiftieth.

CHAPTER 99

Eight years later.

Laura looked out of her kitchen window at her well-kept garden, a large, lush lawn, surrounded by all the colours of summer. The sun shone brightly. Robbie and Rosie were playing table tennis. Jack was reclined in his gravity chair reading a newspaper, he sipped on an iced cold beer. The children were still coming to terms with having a man about the house. They were good kids, thanks to Laura and her mum's efforts and boundless love.

Laura and her sister made up about a year after Jack was incarcerated. Beth was married now with two children of her own, living in a lovely cottage in Devon. Laura and the kids spent a couple of weeks with her each summer.

Jack was released on licence a month ago. This meant he had the inconvenience of reporting to the police station once a month, a small price to pay. He was also warned that if he re-offended for any reason he would have to finish his sentence. Laura knew there was no way Jack was going back. There was nothing in the papers about Jack's early release, Laura knew this wouldn't have been the case if Mrs Rice hadn't of passed away two years earlier.
Jack was genuinely saddened when she told him of her death, he knew he had caused that woman much heart ache.

He only needed one parole hearing before he was set free. Apparently Jack had been an exemplary prisoner, popular with both in-mates and wardens. He spent his time teaching others his woodworking skills and he got himself a degree in business management. Jack had started opening up about his time in prison. This, Laura saw as a great sign. When he was first released he thought everyone was looking at him, pointing accusingly. But in reality people just got on with their lives.

The business had flourished, There were now thirty employees on the pay role. Billy, Michael and Jeff were all directors, soon Jack would be back at the helm where he belonged.
Jack saw Laura looking out and beckoned her to join him, wiggling his beer glass. She indicated to give her five minutes.

It was going to take time for all of them to adapt. Eight years is a hell of a long time. Laura remained looking at Jack, she saw the same vulnerable man she fell in love with all those years ago. Her handsome man was back. She grabbed two beers from the fridge and joined her family in the early evening sunshine.

The End.

Printed in Great Britain
by Amazon